W9-ALN-122

CHEYENNE WAR CRY

The Cheyenne were rising all over the Panhandle in one final, bloody, desperate attempt to wrest back the Texas they called their own. They would be ruthless to get it—raping, torturing, butchering, and slaughtering whoever stood in their way.

Somewhere on the Panhandle lay buried a huge molten cache of lead that meant bullets of victory for the Cheyenne Indians—if they could find it. Only one man knew where it was buried. His name was Stuart Nichols, he was a good man, a just man, with strength in his eyes and steel up his backbone. To find that lead the Cheyenne needed Nichols. First they took his woman . . .

CHEYENNE WAR CRY

Noel M. Loomis

GUNSMOKE

First published by Collins

This hardback edition 2003
by BBC Audiobooks Ltd
by arrangement with
Golden West Literary Agency

ISBN 0 7540 8243 1

British Library Cataloguing in Publication Data available.

TO MARY INKANNISH

A Southern Cheyenne whose birthday is July 14. Her
mother was only ten miles away on the morning when
Custer massacred Black Kettle's village on the Washita;
Mary herself was born within a few days of Custer's
massacre by the Indians on the Little Bighorn. At 83,
Mary is still a pretty Indian girl.

Printed and bound in Great Britain by
Antony Rowe Ltd., Chippenham, Wiltshire

CHAPTER I

IT was the first part of October, 1874. The weather had turned cool after a very hot and dry summer in the Texas Panhandle, and in the Tesecato Canyon, which cut into the eastern edge of the Llano like a long, narrow, ragged wedge, Stuart Nichols walked out from the corrals of the Rocking Seven to study the northwestern sky and wonder if the lessening heat might be a forerunner of rain.

He was a tall, clean-shaven man, and the hair that showed under his big hat was dark brown and his eyes were clear blue. His face had a leathered look that was not unpleasing, and there were crinkles at the corners of his eyes. He observed the clear sky in all directions, felt the warm sun on his arms and shoulders, sniffed the good air. Hearing hoofs from the direction of the mesquite thicket down the creek, he automatically pulled up his gun-belt and turned around.

Anne and Will Schooler rode into the open, and Nichols smiled and waited for them to come up.

Will Schooler was a big, square-faced, red-headed man with a bushy mustache. "Howdy, Nichols."

Nichols nodded. "Will."

Anne said, "Hello, Mr. Nichols."

Nichols looked at her and smiled again. She was a slender woman with light brown hair that was massed at the nape of her neck, under the weather-beaten man's felt hat she wore. But not even the shapeless men's clothes that Will Schooler made her wear could hide her prettiness.

She said, with the hint of a frown between her brown eyes, "You looking for Indians, Mr. Nichols?"

5

"No, ma'am, I was looking for rain—but Indians will do."

She leaned toward him. "You don't like Indians, do you, Mr. Nichols?"

He walked up and rubbed the neck of her little roan gelding. "I hate coyotes, rattlesnakes and Comanches," he said emphatically.

She looked concerned. "You always sound bitter about them, Mr. Nichols."

He said bleakly, "I've seen Indians and I've seen their work. I agree with whoever said a dead Indian is a good Indian."

"They fight the way they have learned, don't they?"

Will Schooler broke in brusquely, impatiently. "Anne, you'd best leave men's affairs to men. Stuart, you seen a stray two-year-old bay with saddle marks?"

Stuart concealed his distaste as he looked at the long-legged bay Schooler was riding. Schooler's selection of horses was no better than most of the things he did that called upon his judgment. Stuart avoided looking at him for a moment as he recalled how many times the hands had expressed their disdain over Schooler's bringing a horse like that into the Texas Panhandle.

"Not this way," he said finally, and looked up, controlling his emotions. "You and Miz Schooler come in and have coffee while you're here, though. Brisket, take their horses."

Brisket came out of the harness-shed, and, behind him, more slowly, came George Nichols, Stuart's white-haired father. He shaded his eyes for a moment against the sun, braced himself on his two crutches and then moved forward laboriously to greet the Schoolers.

Anne dismounted easily, and Brisket took her reins. Will Schooler, getting down from his long-legged bay, stumbled and fell flat on his seat, his legs extended almost under the bay. The horse shied, but Stuart hit its hind quarters with his shoulder and drove it off balance to keep it from stepping on the man's legs.

Schooler got awkwardly to his feet. "Something wrong with those boots," he said. "They're always gettin' caught in the stirrups."

Nobody made an answer. Stuart said, keeping his voice level and casual, "Go on in the house, Will—you and Miz Schooler." He glanced sidewise at Anne and caught her eyes

6

on him. "I have to lay out some work for Brisket," he said, thinking fast.

He turned away and walked into the shed, his father following him on his crutches. Stuart looked out and saw the visitors go through the back door.

His father came inside and took up his place on the milking stool that sat by a saddle on a wooden horse, laying his crutches on the floor.

"You better be watchin' how you look at that woman," his father said.

Stuart said nothing. He pushed his hat back and wiped his forehead with a blue bandanna.

"Only reason you want them to stay and have coffee is so you can sit and look at her."

Stuart glanced down at him. "Wouldn't you?"

"Every man on the ranch would give a day's pay to sit across the table from her at one meal," George said. "Can't say I blame them too much—but that doesn't make it right for you."

"Anne is not the kind who would encourage a man."

"She smiled," George pointed out.

"That's all I want—just to see her smile. And that's all she'd ever do."

George pulled his awl out of the wood and began to work it on a whetstone. "I'll grant you Miz Schooler is a decent, respectable wife—but that don't make no difference either," he insisted. "She's married—and smilin' at a married woman is dangerous."

"Sure," Stuart said more easily. "And you aren't certain what I'm like, are you?" He grinned as George looked up. "I never learned anything in the Texas Rangers about women that I didn't already know. These folks are our neighbors, and I know that."

George looked at him shrewdly. "If you know so much, why did you come running out here?"

Stuart glared at him. There were times when his father was too observant, too shrewd. He pulled his hat down hard and went to the house.

Will was sitting at the homemade table, his big round hat pushed back, blowing on his coffee. Anne glanced at Stuart and then down at her cup. She had taken off her hat. Her hair was almost golden.

7

Stuart sat next to Will and reached for the sugar. "How's the hay in the lower meadow?" he asked.

"Pretty dry—and I don't know if it's the kind that will cure or not."

"Not that tall stuff. You'll have to cut it before it dries up."

Schooler said dubiously, "I suppose I'd better get a couple of the men down there with scythes."

Stuart said, "You could cut that meadow yourself in a week."

Anne looked up and started to say something, but did not. She looked back down at her cup.

"I've got more important things to do than cut hay," said Schooler absently.

Stuart, stirring his coffee, shrugged.

Brisket looked in the back door. "More company, Stuart."

Stuart nodded. "We've got plenty of room."

Anne started to get up.

"More coffee, Miz Schooler?" the cook asked quickly.

"No, thank you." She put on her hat. "We do have to go, Will."

Schooler frowned. "I haven't finished my coffee."

"You're welcome to stay," said Stuart. "It's nothing private as far as I know."

Anne looked at her husband. "We haven't found that horse yet, Will."

He nodded, put his cup to his mouth and threw his head back to drain the cup. Some of the coffee spilled out at one corner of his mouth. He wiped his face with a bandanna, glanced down at his shirt and brushed at the coffee with his hand. "All right, dear—but it's not a very neighborly call, to leave so soon."

Anne said, without looking straight at Stuart, "We're sorry, Mr. Nichols—but you heard Will say we're shorthanded."

"Yes, ma'am. With all the Indian trouble in the Panhandle, we'll all be short-handed for a while, I imagine."

She stopped at the door. "You dislike Indians so much, Mr. Stuart, I'm surprised you didn't join Colonel Miles's column."

He looked at her eyes, trying to see exactly what was behind those words, but her expression told him nothing except that the words had not been idle ones. "We're short-

8

handed like everybody else," he repeated. "A couple of my hands went up to scout for Captain Lyman's wagon train."

"Come along," Will Schooler said impatiently. "Nichols, you mind if we ride on up a ways to look for that horse?"

"Not at all," said Stuart. "Go ahead. Maybe you'll be back for dinner."

"We won't be that long," Anne said.

Stuart rinsed the cup with water from the bucket and set it up on the shelf. "We might have comp'ny for dinner," he told the cook.

"There'll be plenty—if beef and biscuits is good enough for 'em."

"And gravy," said Stuart. He went outside, waved to Will Schooler and Anne, who were making the turn around the clump of willows near the creek, and observed the approaching party with some interest. It was still half a mile away and almost hidden in the tall mesquite, but he could make out three or four moving figures.

"Looks like the Army to me," said Utah Thompson at his elbow.

Stuart glanced at him. "That might be true," he said.

"What for?" asked Utah.

"It's hard to say. The Army moves in ways of its own."

"Maybe they need some beef."

"Miles's subsistence train came down from Camp Supply. It wouldn't be beef."

"You got any idea?" asked Utah.

"An idea? Yes."

"Anything for me to do?"

Stuart looked at the grizzled old mountain man. "Keep your powder dry," he said.

Utah looked at him speculatively, nodded and went back to the harness shed.

Four Army men rode out of the mesquite, all in blue uniforms. The three enlisted men rode bays; the officer, in the lead, rode a chestnut. Stuart raised a hand in cow-country salute and waited for them to ride up.

"Light and stay a while," Stuart said. He raised his voice. "Dusty! Slim!"

His two men came up from behind the corrals to take the horses.

"We've got a feed of oats tied on behind the saddles. Give them about a quart apiece," said the officer, dismounting.

9

"I'm Major Whitehead, U. S. Army, Quartermaster General's Department." The officer was pulling off his gauntleted glove.

"Happy to know you, Major. I'm Stuart Nichols, ramrod of the Rocking Seven." He waved expressively. "Eighty-eight thousand acres of canyon land, lots of good grass, protection from the north winds, springs that so far haven't gone dry." He shrugged. "They may, of course. The Mexicans called it Tesecato—very dry—and I figure they knew what they were doing."

"Looks good now," the major said. "You aren't exactly being flooded out, but at least nothing is burned up yet."

"It probably won't." Stuart led the way to the house. "Sit down, Major, you and your men. Coffee's hot."

The cook poured coffee.

Stuart was fingering the pockets in his black calfskin vest for tobacco.

"Have a cigar," said Whitehead, holding out a crooked stogie.

"Don't mind if I do," said Stuart.

"We come on business," the major said presently, lighting a sulphur match and puffing on his cigar. Then he sent his men into the yard and sat back, his keen blue eyes fixed on Stuart. He looked at the cook. "I'm on Army business—and it's private," he said.

The cook glanced up. Stuart nodded at him. The cook dropped two pieces of mesquite root on the fire, slammed the stove lid on and went outside, wiping his hands on his apron.

Whitehead watched him leave and then turned to Stuart.

"Now, sir, I will summarize for you the military situation in the Panhandle. As you know, there was a large-scale break-out of Indians from the reservations in the western part of the Indian Territory early in the year. There are still from eight hundred to two thousand hostiles somewhere in the Panhandle. These are not all warriors, but a good many of them are—and, of those warriors, many are extremely desperate and savage, and they are well armed."

"So I've heard," observed Stuart.

"We have considerable forces opposed to them: Colonel Miles with twelve companies of Fifth Infantry and Sixth Cavalry, from Fort Dodge, and Colonel Mackenzie up from Fort Griffin with the Fourth Cavalry—both old Indian fighters; Major Price from Fort Union, New Mexico, with three companies of Eighth Cavalry—"

"With which he has done nothing but reconnoiter," said Stuart dryly.

"There has been criticism," the major admitted. "There is also Colonel Davidson from Fort Sill, and a number of smaller units. We are bound to defeat the redskins except for one factor—supplies."

"The Indians live off the country," Stuart noted.

"Precisely. The Indians do; we don't. And there is a factor besides food."

Stuart stared at him. "Ammunition?" he asked.

"Exactly. We must be sure of powder and lead. Our last train from Camp Supply came through, but not without difficulty. Captain Lyman lost a man on that trip, and the Indians stalled the train for three days."

"It's nothing to worry about," said Stuart. "The Indians never carry through an attack, even when they have the advantage."

The major, his curled forefinger holding his cigar, stabbed at the table top with his middle finger. "There is no assurance they won't," he said. "Some of their leaders have shown surprising initiative."

Stuart thought about that a moment. "What do you want me to do?" he asked.

"I am told you know the Llano as well as anybody in the Panhandle."

"As well as anybody except Pablo, who works for me."

"I want you to take five freight wagons to Fort Union and pick up a ton of bar lead and six hundred pounds of powder, along with enough foodstuffs to fill the wagons, and return here to this ranch as fast as possible."

"You said Lyman's train got through," Stuart observed.

"They did not bring enough ammunition in case of a large-scale fight."

"Don't you have more coming?"

"From where?" asked the major. "If Camp Supply or Fort Dodge had had it, we would have gotten it. But Leavenworth does not have enough to spare, so we have to go all the way back to St. Louis."

"Which will take time."

"Too much time—and always the risk the train will be waylaid and the powder and lead fall into the hands of

11

the Indians. I tell you we don't know where these Comanches roam or where they will strike next."

"Do you think you should be telling me this?"

"I can assure you in the strictest confidence, Mr. Nichols —and I say this with the full knowledge of your former service in the Texas Rangers—"

"And my service in the Confederate Army," Stuart said wryly.

Whitehead uttered a sound of exasperation. "A soldier is a soldier no matter what flag he serves under. I also know that you personally hate Indians," he said quietly.

"I'll keep the information to myself," Stuart said. "But the fact is that if the Indians got smart and changed their tactics, and if they were to disrupt your supplies from St. Louis, the columns now in the Panhandle could be in great trouble."

"That's the way it looks to General Sheridan," said Whitehead. "The Army, of course, will pay the usual price—a cent a pound per hundred miles—plus a twenty per cent bonus for extra risk from the Indians now on the Llano, and will guarantee your physical losses."

Stuart nodded. "Fair enough. You said five wagons? Why not send just two wagons—or even one?"

"With Stone Calf of the Cheyennes and Quanah Parker of the Quahadi Comanches out there?" The major shook his head. "No, sir. That's just the thing we're afraid of. If they saw one lone wagon they would know it to be ammunition. It is entirely possible they would be able to rally their warriors in an all-out attack, and would not only interfere with our supply but would augment theirs enough to prolong the campaign for months—if not actually to defeat us."

Stuart studied him over the cigar. "You think it's possible the Indians might win?"

Whitehead expostulated. "Man for man, the Indians are as good fighters as our men; they are far better subsisters—and they have us outnumbered. What better odds can you ask?"

"It sounds as if you're whipped."

Whitehead said earnestly, "Mr. Nichols, the Indians, with all their inability to fight as a unit of an army, have whipped us several times. More than once, with the very limited forces allowed us by Congress, we have been very nearly beaten off the Midwestern plains—and it is conceivable that this might be the time they would finish the job. I am very serious, Mr.

12

Nichols, in saying that this is a more important campaign than many persons realize. We hope, of course, that it will go in the usual manner—but General Sheridan is not a man to hope blindly."

Stuart nodded. "He's a good soldier—and he knows what he's up against." He looked up. "All right. It's October and a bad time of year to leave the ranch short-handed. A norther could come up and wipe us out. But I'll go." He rolled the cigar on his lips. "A ton of lead will kill a lot of Indians. I'll go."

CHAPTER II

WHITEHEAD studied him for a moment and nodded slightly, looking relieved. Stuart got up, went to the stove and got the coffee pot. He filled their cups and put the pot back, then sat down and reached for the sugar crock.

"When can you start?" asked Whitehead.

Stuart, thinking, said slowly, "It's better than two hundred miles—let's say eight days to get there, ten to come back with loaded wagons." He looked up. "I'll start in the morning, Major."

Whitehead beamed. "Thank you, sir. I was hoping that would be your answer."

"I know you were," Stuart said dryly.

"I take it you have wagons, horses and harness."

"I have wagons. We won't use horses—mules are better up there when the water holes go dry."

Whitehead was on his feet. "Then, Mr. Nichols, I leave it in your hands—with a strong admonition to say nothing to anyone of the situation which I have described to you in confidence."

"I will say that we are going after supplies. My men will assume that a part of those supplies will be powder and lead, and I won't deny it. But I will keep the rest of it to myself."

"And, above all else, you will keep in mind the very severe hazard to all Army forces if the Indians get that powder and lead, and you will take every possible precaution to keep it out of their hands."

"That goes without saying, major."

Stuart went outside and rescued the cook from a lifting

contest with the sergeant and two privates. "Four extra men for dinner," he said. "Don't hold back on the biscuits."

The cook grinned. "Do my best," he promised.

Stuart went out to the harness shed and told Utah about the trip.

"We'll take five wagons, thirty-six mules, which will give us an extra team, and we'll need five drivers. You and I can trade off. We'll need Pablo, Brisket Smith, and Dusty—" He stopped. "I hate to take more away from the ranch. Maybe—"

"Maybe this is your man coming up now," said Utah. "John Fisher."

Stuart looked at the big, whiskered man riding across the yard. "He never drove for me," he said, considering. "And he doesn't like Pablo."

"Well," said Utah, "maybe Fisher won't drive anyway."

Fisher rode his big bay into the yard, and Stuart stepped out to meet him. "How are things on the LHJ?" Stuart asked casually.

"Good enough," said Fisher.

Stuart glanced at him. Fisher had curiously watery-looking blue eyes. He always had a week's growth of beard, and he wore an old hat that had come out of the Mexican War. But there was a feeling of brute power about him that a person could not ignore. "Light," Stuart said without much enthusiasm.

Fisher dismounted. "Saw the Army people comin' up here," he said without preliminary. "Figgered you'd be freightin' for 'em."

"Possible," said Stuart.

"Like to hire out as driver," said Fisher.

Stuart said, "I figured you'd be pretty busy on the LHJ."

"Sure—but I could mighty well use a few dollars of cash money."

He said it almost humbly, and Stuart was touched. Fisher was not a man anybody took to, and he kept to himself, but nobody had stopped to think whether or not he might be hard put for money.

"Sure, I can use a driver. We start in the morning."

"Thanks." Fisher got back in the saddle. Then he looked around. "Nice place you got here," he said. "A lot more water up here than I get down below. Grass is burning up down there." He wheeled the big bay and rode off at a lope.

Utah took a big bite from a chew in his hip pocket.

15

Stuart said thoughtfully, "He acted like a man that wanted a job."

"A rattlesnake don't change his poison," Utah said sourly, "even when he sheds his skin."

Stuart looked at Utah. "You've always had it in for Fisher."

Utah shook his head slowly. "I never liked his looks."

"Of course he's always been too close to the Indians—and that looks bad for him."

"It ain't that," said Utah. "I been close to the Indians too. I had a Ute squaw back in the fifties. So that don't cut no ice. It's the *way* he was with them. He was a *comanchero* trader—one of the worst. He took money from husbands and fathers to buy white women captives from the Indians—and turned around and sold the women to other tribes, and got more money to try it again. He's a half outlaw with a bunch of ex-outlaws workin' for him down there on the LHJ."

"Maybe they're trying to get started right."

Utah snorted. "I know a lot of his tricks. He took to dealing with Stone Calf when the Cheyennes come down here, and, if he was still trading, I'd swear he had plenty to do with this break-out."

"What can he gain out of it?"

"He could make money hand over fist supplying the Indians."

"He isn't trading—is he?"

"I'd hate to bet on it," Utah said darkly. "Did you see the greedy look in his face when he mentioned how good your grass looked?"

Stuart said casually, "Natural."

"No, it ain't. Jealous, maybe, but not greedy."

Stuart sent Brisket and Dusty to round up the mules and went back toward the harness-shed. "He's our neighbor," he reminded Utah, "and we're duty-bound to help him get along if we can do it." They walked together behind the shed. "You better look over the harness," said Stuart. "I'll inspect the wagons."

"If the wagons wasn't made out of bois d'arc," said Utah, "they'da shrunk to the size of a small pecan a year ago. When them two git back with the mules, you better send 'em to give me a hand with the neat's-foot. This harness is dryin' up."

"All right." Stuart looked to the northwest, but the two hands were already out of sight around the bend of the canyon. Anne and Will Schooler were trotting back. He straightened up, took a step in that direction, then remembered what his father had said. He considered it a moment, realized that his father was right and went back to the wagons.

He saw no split tongues or cracked reaches, and the wheels seemed solid enough. He'd sling an extra tongue under one of the wagon boxes, and they could carry a couple of extra wheels and axles.

He saw that a couple of the water kegs slung on the sides of the wagons were dry and the staves had separated; if they were soaked in the creek overnight, they would be all right by morning. The others would have to be emptied and refilled with fresh water. He'd put Dusty and Brisket on that as soon as they got back with the mules. The neat's-footing could be done by lantern light. He'd have to check with the cook to see what they could take with them for food—probably beans, rice, coffee, bacon and cornmeal.

The outfit as a whole should be in fair shape, for he had only been back ten days from hauling a trainload of wool from Las Vegas to Dodge.

He looked in each wagon bed—the tarps were in the shed, and the boxes were empty except for shovels and grubbing hoes. They would need a couple of brass kettles. He took hold of a wheel and tried to shake it. The wheel itself was solid, but it sounded gritty on the axle; that meant a job of greasing twenty axles before they started, but it shouldn't be a bad job with empty wagons. He thought—

"Mr. Nichols, may I ask you something?"

He straightened up and looked down at Anne. He hadn't heard her walk in. "Yes, ma'am," he said.

"It's about Will."

He glanced around. "Where's Will now?" he asked.

"He had a touch of the sun, and I persuaded him to stop in at the ranch house and sit down for a few minutes while I came out here to tell you we didn't find any trace of the horse."

She looked small and feminine even in the bulky, ill-fitting clothes she wore, and he took a deep breath. "Do you mind if I ask you a personal question, ma'am?"

She looked straight at him.

"Why don't you ever wear women's clothes? I never saw you dressed up."

"I—well, Will thinks it's more becoming this way. He says dresses are not modest on horseback."

"You must have ridden sidesaddle," said Stuart.

She laughed ineffectually. "Well, you know how husbands are."

"Maybe not," he said. "My mother died when I was little, and I never lived in a house where there was a woman."

"I'm sorry," she said softly. "Some day, I hope—"

"Some day I'm going to change that," he said, looking at her.

She glanced at the gloves in her hands. "I came out here to ask a favor of you."

"I'll be glad to grant it," he said immediately.

She laughed self-consciously. "It's about Will. It seems that most of my talk is about Will."

"I have noticed that."

She looked up suddenly. "We met your men rounding up the mules, and Will spoke of asking you for a job driving."

He knew what was coming. "What do you want me to tell him?" he asked finally.

"Tell him no. Tell him anything—but don't let him drive."

He looked at her steadily. "Why don't you want him to go?"

She said, looking away, "He's clumsy. I'm afraid if he tries to drive a wagon to Fort Union and back he might get hurt."

He asked with a shade of disbelief, "You care that much about him, ma'am?"

She faced him squarely, her head erect, her face in the brilliant sunlight. Her eyes did not evade his, and she was no longer embarrassed. "Mr. Nichols," she said, "Will Schooler may be clumsy and inept, but he is my husband. I will remember that—and I suggest you remember it also."

Will Schooler walked across the yard a few minutes later. "Nichols, I'd like to hire out for this trip."

Stuart looked at him curiously. "What for, Will? You don't need the money, do you?"

"Everybody needs money," said Schooler, "but that ain't it, Nichols. It seems like I'm always sittin' at home when things happen. I'd like to be around sometimes. I want to do my share of the work and take my share of the risks."

Stuart said thoughtfully, "I'll tell you, Will. I picked this

18

crew with the idea that somebody real steady would be left in the Tesecato, because the Cheyennes just might pick this place to raid first. I figured my dad on the Rocking Seven and you on the Bar M. I'd consider it a favor if you'd stay put on this trip, Will."

Will Schooler accepted it, but not happily. "I'm always the one to stay at home and hold the fort," he noted, looking away. He added as he turned, "I suppose I'll have to do something drastic to prove I'm no tenderfoot on the plains."

CHAPTER III

THE men got to bed about midnight and were up long before the sun. The Comanche moon filled the canyon with a mellow light that was almost as good as daylight to work by.

Fisher rode in as they were catching up the mules. Stuart said, "You can leave your saddle and bridle in the shed and turn your horse loose. He'll drift back home, I imagine."

"I'm taking my horse with me," said Fisher.

Stuart looked at him and got a glimmer of the hard-headedness that Utah didn't like. "There will be only one saddle horse on the trip," Stuart said quietly, "and I'm riding that."

"We'll have no way of getting away if there is an Indian attack," said Fisher. "You want to get us scalped?"

"If there is an attack," Stuart said, "I expect every man to stay and defend the train unless he wants a shot in the back."

Fisher said belligerently, "You threatenin' me?"

"That's a rule of the train," Stuart said. "You go by the rule or you go back home."

Fisher studied him in the moonlight. "Who's makin' up these rules?" he demanded.

"It's my train. I make the rules," Stuart said quickly.

He waited for Fisher's reaction. If it was going to be this way, he hoped Fisher would back out now.

Finally Fisher laughed awkwardly. "All right, Nichols, it's your show—but don't say I didn't warn you."

Stuart said, "Hitch up your team to the number five wagon there and get ready to move out. You are responsible for your own wagon from now on. They've been checked and greased

20

and the water kegs filled, but you'd better examine everything to see for yourself."

Stuart walked away, went to every water keg and thumped them to make sure they were full. When he got to the front, Utah was sitting in the seat, holding the reins. The wagons— all without bows or canvas—looked sleek and trim in the moonlight, and the six-mule teams stood patiently, waiting for the whip-cracks that would start the trip.

Fisher was still harnessing up. Stuart walked back. One of Fisher's wheel mules had stepped through the breeching, and Fisher was swearing and trying to get the mule to move.

"It's not necessary to cuss these mules," said Stuart. "We all do it, but it's a poor way to start out the day. How did that happen anyway? That mule can mighty near harness himself."

Fisher looked up, his face partly hidden in the shadow of his hat. "You gave me the worst team of the lot," he said.

Stuart's answer was cold. "You've still got time to change your mind."

Fisher seemed to hesitate, and then he said, with that strange humility that indicated to Stuart that the man really needed the few dollars he would make, "I can't afford it."

"Then get your team ready and we'll pull out."

He rode back to the front.

A moment later, Fisher climbed into the driver's seat. Stuart said to Utah, "All right."

Utah's long whip cracked over the lead mules' heads, and Utah began to talk. The mules walked forward easily under the almost empty wagons. The big wheels with their four-inch-wide iron tires rumbled hollowly down the grass slope to the creek, splashed through and started up the other side.

"Hold them down," Stuart told Utah.

Utah growled something Stuart could not make out, but which ended, "Bunch of damn' jugheads!"

The five wagons strung out in a long line. The six extra mules were tied on a lead line behind the last wagon. Each man had a bedroll in his own wagon, plus rifle, six-shooter and cartridges. Stuart sat by the trail as the wagons turned to their right and started up the road to the point where they would be able to get over the Caprock.

Fisher called to him: "How long do I have to ride back here in the dirt?"

"The wagons will rotate every day," Stuart shouted above

the rumbling of the empty boxes. "You'll be number four tomorrow."

He checked the trailing mules and saw that they were moving along easily. All of his mules were well broke to freighting, and he seldom had trouble. All was quiet at the moment. The sky began to lighten over the Caprock in the east. Four coyotes stood right at the spot where the sun would come up and watched curiously as the train followed the winding trail up the canyon.

Stuart turned back and rode to the front, past Utah's team. It was now the quiet, cool hour of early morning, sweet and fresh like the dew on an acre of bluestem grass. Bobwhites called to one another somewhere up ahead, and their throaty whistles seemed toned down for fear of disturbing the silence of the dawn. Five antelope got up from beside the creek, unseen in the small growth of willows and cottonwoods until they floated suddenly into view. Then they shot ahead with their amazing, silent speed until they were near the end of the Tesecato; but, before they were boxed in, they turned in a fast, graceful half circle and floated by the train just under the Caprock on the far side, out of rifle shot, white rumps hazy in the shadow of the cliff.

Stuart's gray shied suddenly as half a hundred quail zoomed up without warning and exploded into flight up the canyon. They were well grown, and Stuart was satisfied that there had been plenty of water in the Tesecato all summer, for quail did not thrive away from water. He came upon black bear sign and thought there might be a den in a clump of cedars up under the Caprock on the west side.

The sun came over the rim then and poured its golden light into the canyon. At that time of day it was almost as mellow as the light of the full moon. And still the world was quiet, except for the occasional snort of a mule, the rumble of wagons, the creak of leather harness, the jingle of trace chains, the soft plop of hoofs in the sod.

Up ahead the road turned to the left and started uphill. Stuart stood the gray at one side and watched them all start the climb. Brisket was behind Utah, Dusty was next and Pablo was fourth. Stuart rode alongside Pablo and asked, "That bay mule gettin' along all right?"

"Seguro," said Pablo.

"I'll bet you'll be glad to get to Fort Union and Little Chihuahua."

Pablo grinned. "I know a woman there—she's little but *simpática*—black eyes, mmm! Big in the *tetas,* quick in the hind end. You know?" He shivered as he thought about it.

Stuart grinned. "How about her husband?"

"I've never seen him," Pablo said thoughtfully. "She must have one, though, with six *niñas.*"

"Not necessarily."

"*Cómo, señor?*"

"Never mind. *Es cosa de Méjico.*"

He watched Fisher make the turn to the next higher level, and the train traveled now with the dropoff to its left. They would go around the far end of the canyon—which was not the main canyon of the Tesecato but a dry canyon to the south of it—and then go in a steep climb back toward the southeast. It was easy enough going up with empty wagons; coming down with full loads would not be so easy.

Stuart turned off the road to the left and dismounted. He climbed the steep slope on foot; the gray followed, pawing for a foothold, straining its neck forward to maintain its balance. A lot of horses would not have made that climb, but the gray was like a bloodhound—and it had been up that trail before.

They regained the narrow one-way road and waited for the wagons. The road was wide enough for one wagon only; the Army had done most of the work of cutting it into the Caprock, making a tiny shelf for travel. The rain had washed it pretty badly, and in places the ruts were over a foot deep. The wagons would have to stay in the ruts, for there was not room against the cliff to ride the ridges and there was little more than a foot between the left-hand ridge and the edge.

Stuart sat on a rock just off the edge and rolled a cigarette, while the gray got its breath back and began to crop at tufts of grass among the rocks, avoiding the catclaw and purple loco weed. Stuart watched the wagons round the turn below. The sun was up full now, and its heat poured down into the closed-off canyon.

The wagons got around the bend and straightened up on the long, steep climb. The mules' necks were in their collars, their heads nodding as they made the pull. Stuart got to his feet and walked up the road ahead of them, leading the gray.

They came out on top of the Llano, a vast tableland, flat and treeless as far as an antelope could see—and that was pretty far.

Stuart spent some time scrutinizing the horizon to north, south, and west and studying the land in between. There was nothing bigger than a bear grass to hide Indians, but he knew how many Comanches could conceal themselves behind one bear grass, so he watched carefully. He saw no telltale wisp of dust against the sky.

This was the train's most vulnerable point—reaching the top. At this point they could be cut in two, and those below would have little defense.

Utah Thompson talked his team out on top, using his whip to keep up a crackling fire over their heads. He pulled a hundred yards from the edge and stopped, wrapped his reins around the foot iron and got down.

Brisket drew up beside him, took a quick look at the horizon and got down. Dusty drew up, then Pablo.

Fisher was slow, and Stuart went to find out why. His lead pair was lathering at the mouth. Stuart waited for him to get on top. "Don't work so hard at driving," he said. "Those mules know what to do. Quit sawing at them!"

Fisher glowered at him, but drove alongside Pablo's wagon and got down.

Stuart said loudly, "We'll give them a five-minute breather. Drink out of your own canteens, but don't touch the kegs. We'll hit water about mid-afternoon, if we're lucky."

"When do we eat?" asked Brisket.

"We'll stop for grub about ten or eleven o'clock, and let the mules graze till two. Then we'll drive late this evening."

Stuart had never had this crew before, but he was fairly well satisfied that Fisher was the only one who showed signs of not being harness-broke. He couldn't quite figure the man out, either. Did he want to be contrary or had he just never learned to get along with anybody but Indians? And why didn't he show more savvy about mules?

Pablo sat down cross-legged; like most Mexicans in cow work, he did not wear a straw hat but chose the usual felt hat of the cowhand. He felt in his shirt pocket for tobacco but found none and started up.

"Here," said Brisket, "use mine."

All of them but Fisher were sitting around; Fisher was back by the wagons.

"No," said Pablo. "I got my own." He dusted the seat of his pants.

Utah said, "Aw, sit down. Here, have a chew!"

Pablo shook his head. *"Gracias, no."* He started for his wagon.

The gray was ground-hitched, and Stuart squatted down with the others.

Utah said, "I don't smell no Indians up here."

"You can't smell 'em that far," said Dusty, a wizened little man of indeterminate age.

"If I can't, my nigh swing mule can. That dun spots an Indian farther'n a thirsty steer smells water, and I can tell by the way she twitches her ears which tribe it is."

"Aw, now—"

Suddenly they were interrupted by a commotion over by Pablo's wagon.

"Caramba!" sang out Pablo.

"You dirty, stinkin'—"

Stuart was on his feet, running, the minute he heard Fisher's heavy voice thick with curses and Pablo's excited Spanish. He could hear sounds of a scuffle as he ran, and he rounded the rear wheel of Pablo's wagon, seized Fisher by the shoulder and spun him away like a big top.

Pablo was standing with a dagger pointed outward. "He steal my water," Pablo said, his black eyes flashing. "I weel cut him up."

Fisher said harshly, "He's a dirty, stinkin'—"

Stuart said coldly, "If you are going to make this trip, you will not refer to Pablo that way any more." He looked at the rope that held the canvas cover on the keg; the rope ends hung loose. "I told you to drink out of your canteen. Why were you in the kegs?"

"I tapped the keg," Fisher said, "and it sounded empty. I thought I'd better see."

Stuart said coldly, "You've been up here on the Llano long enough to know that a man can get shot for fooling with somebody else's water." He glanced at Pablo and saw the bruise on Pablo's cheekbone.

"You've no call to be grandpappy of the outfit," said Fisher morosely.

"I'm paying the wages; I'll name the tune."

Fisher looked at him; Stuart could not read his eyes.

"I don't like Mexicans," Fisher said finally.

"You knew that when you started."

"I been eatin' his dust all the way."

Stuart said, "You're going to eat somebody's dust four days

out of five." He struck at the big iron tire with his gloves. "I don't want trouble with you, Fisher. If this kind of thing is going to keep up, I'll pay you for a day's work now and you can go back to the ranch."

Unexpectedly, Fisher became contrite. "I'll behave," he said. "I told you I needed the money, and I still do."

"All right. Act like it—and stay off Pablo. He's got a lot of friends in this crew."

Fisher didn't answer. He went to the far side of his wagon, sat on his heels and started to roll a cigarette.

Pablo retied the rope around the canvas over the head of the keg, then got his tobacco and went back to join the others. Utah said in a low voice, "There's somethin' fishy in that spiel he makes about needing money. That ain't what's behind him at all."

"Why should he say it, then?"

"Because he's heard that you can't turn down anybody who says he needs money."

"That's not much of an explanation. Why would he want to go on the trip at all?"

Utah said darkly, "You'll find out by the time we get back."

CHAPTER IV

THEY made good time across the endless prairies of the Llano. There was a trail, but it didn't matter much whether they followed it exactly or not, for one part of the prairie was like another. The trail wasn't well worn enough to be a road, so for a time the wagons traveled abreast across the prairie. The grass sometimes made bumpy going, sometimes smooth. But the mules pulled well, and Stuart saw thirty miles a day turned off until they reached the western Caprock and went down into the breaks of New Mexico. There once again they traveled in single file. Pablo knew the water holes in that area better than Stuart. If Fisher knew them, he did not reveal it. Nevertheless, they managed to camp near water except for one night. They rolled into Fort Union about sundown one afternoon, with the sun blood-red and the western sky stabbed with great patches of red and gold, purple and blue.

By the time they pulled into the yard, Old Truchas Peak loomed up to the west and the sun had gone behind it, causing a dazzling halo to cover the western sky.

Dusty, who seldom spoke, said, "It sure is pretty."

Utah, still sitting in the seat, told Stuart, "There's times I'm almost ashamed of bein' a heathen."

Stuart nodded. He knew what they felt. The only thing he didn't like was the indication of dust in the air, far to the west. Somewhat worried, he turned the gray to the commandant's office.

The quartermaster had a list of supplies that he had received by telegraph. "We'll load you up tomorrow, Mr. Nichols. We're a little short-handed; part of our forces are with Major Price and the rest are on patrol in this area, so I don't think we will ask the men to load five or six tons of goods tonight."

"All right with me," said Stuart. "We'll move out before daylight day after tomorrow."

"That will be fine. You can leave your wagons and mules with the stable sergeant. He'll feed them and take care of them."

"I'll see if I can keep track of the men enough to make a good start back."

"There's plenty of entertainment, but it's mostly on the rough side."

"My men are not troublemakers, but they can take care of themselves."

Stuart went back to the men. "You can sleep here in the barracks if you want," he said. "Whatever you do, be here at three o'clock in the morning day after tomorrow."

Utah grinned. "Too bad I ain't got time to get down to Santa Fe or up to Taos. I know lots of people there."

"You mean lots of wimmen," said Brisket.

Utah shrugged. "Ain't wimmen people?"

Stuart gave them five dollars apiece. Unexpectedly, Fisher said he had two dollars and would not want more, preferring to save his pay until he got back. He had behaved fairly decently since the incident of Pablo's water keg, and Stuart thought better of him.

He felt better, that is, until that night, when he and Utah were sitting in a saloon outside of the fort area drinking Taos lightning. It was as clear as plain alcohol, and had almost as much wallop.

Brisket, Dusty, Pablo, and Fisher all were absent on business of their own.

"What do you suppose your friend Fisher did as soon as we got away from the fort?" asked Utah.

Stuart grinned at him. "Why should I guess when you know?"

"He hired a saddle horse and took off northeast. I'd say you lost yourself a driver."

Stuart frowned. "I don't make any sense out of it. He wouldn't make this trip as a driver just to get to Fort Union."

"You know what's northeast?"

28

"Bent's Fort, I suppose."

"Sure." Utah's deep-set eyes gleamed in his leathery face. "And maybe Indians. Nobody knows where the Indians are unless it's Fisher."

"What could he tell them?"

"He could tell them we're taking back five wagonloads —and there's sure to be ammunition in the wagons."

Stuart shrugged. "It doesn't figure out. What could the Indians possibly pay him for that information? What would he gain?"

"Squaws, maybe."

Stuart grunted. "I wouldn't have one of those stinkin'—"

Utah said dryly, "You sound like Fisher."

Stuart looked up, startled. "Then I better quit saying that."

"And thinkin', too."

"What I think is my business," Stuart said sharply.

All the men but Fisher and Pablo showed up the next afternoon as the soldiers finished packing the wagons. They looked a little bleary but well-satisfied. Pablo came in about dark. "It was difficult to leave," he said. "Sometimes I think I move to Fort Union."

Utah snorted. "You'd be stumbling over soldiers and everything else."

"I sure hate to leave her," Pablo said dreamily.

They got to bed after Stuart and Utah had checked harness, mules, wagons and the lashed tarpaulins over the loads. All the lead—2,200 pounds in bars—was in Utah's wagon. The gunpowder—600 pounds in canisters—was in Brisket's wagon, along with hogsheads of flour and dried apples. There were five sacks of shelled corn as emergency feed for the mules.

Stuart had slept that afternoon, and now it looked like a good thing he had, for it was after midnight and Fisher had not shown up.

Utah pulled a bottle out of his pocket after they got into the barracks. Pablo and Brisket and Dusty were all asleep. Brisket was flat on his back, snoring lustily; Dusty was curled up, making no sound; Pablo was tossing a little and kept saying, *"Chiquita, chiquita!"*

"There's two drinks left—one for you and one for me," said Utah, and passed the bottle. . . .

Stuart awoke in pitch blackness. He got up and walked

29

outside in his stockinged feet to look at the stars. It was three o'clock, and the air from the mountains was cold. He shivered and went back to pull on his boots. He touched Utah's shoulder. "All right, old-timer, let's head for the Tesecato."

Pablo woke up easily. Dusty jumped violently when Stuart spoke to him, and came awake rubbing his eyes. He had to shake Brisket hard; Brisket gave three or four snorts and suddenly swung up and said, "Damn' short nights they have in New Mexico." He yawned.

They went outside. "We'll lead the gray," Stuart said, "and I'll drive the—"

"Nichols?" said a harsh voice.

Stuart turned to see a man on horseback against the starlit sky. He recognized the floppy-brimmed hat. "Fisher?"

He knew Fisher was grinning sardonically when he asked, "You said three o'clock, didn't you?"

"That's right," Stuart said shortly. "Give the sergeant fifty cents to take care of your horse. We're moving out."

Fisher said softly, "All right, Nichols."

Stuart wheeled before he could check himself. Utah was right; Fisher had something up his sleeve. Stuart said, "You'll drive the same wagon. Your place to start is number two. Pablo is ahead of you."

They pulled out long before daylight, and when the sun came up they were headed southeast to hit the road that would ascend the Caprock on the New Mexico side. They would have several days of rough country before they got back to the Caprock.

Stuart rode alongside Utah in the number three wagon. "One thing I don't like too much," he said.

"That sunset?" asked Utah.

"It looked like dust in the air."

"We had it again last night, too."

"Storm coming up out of Arizona Territory, maybe," said Stuart. "If it is, it'll catch us in the middle of the Llano."

By noon that day, the wind was increasing in force.

"If it gets much stronger," said Utah, "it'll pick up sand—and we'll be in for it."

But the wind went down that afternoon, and Stuart felt relieved, though he did not like the look of the sky.

The western half of the horizon, extending to the zenith overhead, was splashed with gorgeous masses of color—

intermingled layers of red and orange, purple and gold, green and fiery yellow.

"*Es muy bonito,*" Pablo said reverently. He paused in examining the lashings of the tarpaulins that covered his load.

Stuart nodded. He looked a moment longer and then turned away abruptly. For some reason, at that moment the trip across the Llano looked unaccountably long. The miles stretched out ahead, and there was weather and Indians to consider.

They circled the wagons and prepared for the night. He rolled up in his blanket and went to sleep.

But they were not on the Llano yet. The next day they kept on through the breaks of New Mexico, the going much slower. Twenty miles a day would be good time, and Stuart consulted with Pablo and rode far ahead to scout the water holes.

The third night, still below the Caprock, they camped dry, and he saw to it that the mules were not allowed to graze, for an animal without water got along better without feed.

Along toward morning, the mules, picketed in a sandy draw with only a few small wild plum bushes to forage on, began to bray. Stuart heard the first one and was awake immediately. He got up, pulled on his boots and walked quietly around the wagons. He heard the smooth rustle of canvas against canvas, and ducked in between two wagons. The moon was behind a cloud, but there was still enough light to see by.

With his pistol in his hand, he went around the end of Utah's wagon and saw a figure he could not identify. He said in a low voice, "Put 'em up!"

The man hesitated and then turned his head, and Stuart recognized the floppy hat of John Fisher. The man said, "You scared me."

Stuart said suspiciously, "What are you doing with that canvas?"

"I wasn't sleepin', and I thought I heard an animal or something in this wagon."

Stuart said, "The best thing you can possibly do is keep your fingers out of every wagon but your own."

Fisher shrugged and walked to his own wagon. He crawled underneath, sat on his bed and pulled off his boots, pulled the blanket up and lay down.

Stuart walked around the mules, knowing that their braying would carry for miles. This was not, however, the country of the four tribes now at war on the plains—the Kiowas, Southern Cheyennes, Comanches, and Arapahoes—and he did not seriously consider Indians. Undoubtedly Fisher had been looking for the powder and lead, for he had not been present when the wagons were loaded, as had been the others. Exactly what good that information would do him Stuart didn't know.

The next day, about noon, they hit water. He let the mules drink and graze and drink again, and toward evening they moved on for a couple of hours.

They followed a wagon trail alongside a shallow lake filled with stumps, and that night their fire filled the little valley with the rich fragrance of burning cedar. The next day they went through the Angosturas—the Narrows—and finally went over a low but rugged mountain and ascended the Caprock itself. Once again they were on the broad and almost limitless plains of the Llano.

That night they camped at Las Escarbadas—the Scrapings—where they dug holes in the sand of a dry water course and dipped out bucketful after bucketful of water as it collected in the holes.

"It ain't so good," said Utah after supper. "There was water on top of the ground when we came west."

"The wind may have blown it down," said Stuart.

The wind was up again the next morning, and they had to spread a tarpaulin across the side of a wagon to build their breakfast fire behind. Utah always built a regular stove and chimney with the big buffalo chips, but the wind would have torn it down out in the open.

Stuart stood against the tarpaulin, the wind whipping his pant legs behind him. His black calfskin vest, which had no buttons, flapped when the wind caught hold of the open sides.

He held his hat with one hand and looked into the west. "This has been building up for a week," he said. "I don't think it's going to be over right away."

Utah looked back toward New Mexico. "It started in the due west," he said.

"Let's hope it stays there, for there'll be sand on it in a couple of hours and we won't be able to see a thing."

"Take your bearings on the sun," said Utah.

Brisket, holding onto his hat, spoke up. "I seen these

storms before. The sun'll be covered by noon. And the prairies all look alike—millions of acres. You can't tell one from another."

Stuart spoke loud against the wind. "We could sit here and wait it out, but that might be two weeks."

Dusty joined them. "I think we can find the Tesecato," he said.

Stuart looked at him. "You never been on the Llano in a real sandstorm," he observed.

They finished breakfast, harnessed up the mules and pulled out with the wind. By that time, the first small grains of sand were being carried on the wind. The sand traveled level with the ground at forty or fifty miles an hour and stung hard when it hit a man's skin. Stuart was glad they weren't heading into it.

By the time they had been on the road for an hour, the sun was blotted out. The air was filled with sand, and, as the wind increased in force, the size of the sand particles increased, too. The mules' ears were bent forward all the time, as if they were broken. Pablo lost his hat, and it sailed out of sight in seconds. Pablo started after it, but Stuart sent him back. "You'll get lost out there!" he shouted. "Stay with your wagon."

Pablo's eyes were wide as he looked up at Stuart, and his *"Si, señor,"* was lost in the steady, ever-rising howl of the wind.

Pablo went back to his wagon, bent far over against the wind. He climbed into the seat and tied a red bandanna around his head.

The wind was exerting so much force against the rear of the wagons that it was hard to keep the mules from trotting, but Stuart rode back down the line and told all the drivers to keep their mules at a walk and in line. They were not to spread out. He knew that he could keep the gray at a walk, and, with the mules behind him, it would be easier to hold them down. If they should be allowed to run on the prairie, there could easily be a runaway that might result in a smashed-up wagon.

By noon the prairie looked the same in all directions.

"I never knew it could be so much the same," said Dusty.

"You'll say that a hundred times before we get home," Stuart assured him.

It was hard to talk at all, with the sound of the wind

roaring through the wheels and against the wagon boxes. The air was so filled with sand they could not see a wagon over forty feet away.

Stuart rode alongside Utah, who looked at him and bit off a chew. "Where we campin' tonight?" he shouted.

"Wherever we stop."

Utah put the plug back in his pocket and shouted again, "We ought have some bows and put up some canvas. We wouldn't need no mules."

Stuart nodded. He had tied his chin straps under his chin, and now, though the wind had blown his hat out of all resemblance to the shape it had had, it stayed on. Utah was driving bare-headed, his gray-black hair over his eyes half the time. Brisket had tied his chin straps, and Fisher had stuffed his old hat in a corner of the wagon.

Stuart rode on out ahead. He did not dare to scout beyond visible distance, for he could lose the train in a couple of minutes. He dropped back again to speak to Utah. "D'you think an Indian could trail us in this wind?"

Utah said judiciously, "Not a Ute, probably—but I figger the Plains Indians could find us if they wanted to."

Stuart rode on ahead. About all he could do was run before the wind and hope it did not change direction too much. When he came to a draw, they would all follow it down and try to find a place where they could dig for water. . . .

They hit no draws that day. They continued to skim over the endless, flat prairie. This was the way they had come, as far as Stuart could tell, but it looked altogether different, flattened out as it was by the wind.

Their breath was jerked out of them when they turned to face the wind, and the sand scoured their faces when they looked back. The back ends of the wagons looked as if they had been scoured with grit, and nowhere was there any protection from the corrosive action of the sand.

Above, the sky was like a gray bowl. There was no indication of the sun.

Stuart let the mules go on past noon. After what he thought was a very good day, he stopped the wagons and lined them up in a column of twos broadside to the wind, putting Utah's wagon at the apex. The lead inside would hold it down, and it would help to break the force for the others. They built a fire in the lee of the wagons after one wagon sheet, used to protect the fire, had been torn loose from its grommets by a gust of changing wind and had sailed instantly out of sight above them.

Stuart had broken open a sack of corn and fed the mules half of it, holding back half a sack for morning. He emptied two kegs watering them.

"We might be up here a long time," Utah warned.

"The more reason," Stuart said, "for keeping the mules in good shape. We can't pull the wagons by ourselves."

Brisket, looking toward the trail behind them with narrowed eyes, said, "We should hit water tomorrow, shouldn't we?"

"No telling," said Stuart. "All a man can be sure of in this wind is that we're heading east."

Dusty was making cornbread and frying bacon. Stuart got a jug of molasses. "Everybody feed up," he said.

They made their beds down where the fire had been, leaving the canvas in place. Stuart watched the men. Human nerves might be the first to go under the screeching, demonic wind, which never let up. It did not come in gusts. The pressure was there constantly, until it became a sort of vacuum in which the tearing force of the wind was normal, and anything else would have been terrifying.

Stuart slept fitfully, getting up twice to look at the mules.

At last it was daylight. Whether it was dawn or midmorning he could not tell, but it was no longer night.

Brisket opened his eyes, looked around and pulled on his boots. Stuart was making coffee. Pablo, next to Brisket, awoke and sat up straight. *"Caramba!"* he said, and Stuart would not have heard the words if he had not been immediately downwind from Pablo. "Why do we leave the Tesecato?"

Brisket walked out to look at the mules, but in a moment he was back. He bent down to shout in Stuart's ear. "You know we set the wagons broadside to the wind last night?"

Stuart nodded.

Brisket said, "Either the wagons is moved or the wind is changed, because she's blowin' almost on the tailgates now!"

CHAPTER V

STUART talked it over with Utah. They had no choice but to try to maintain a course with the wind blowing broadside against them. It might change a dozen times during the day, but they would have no way of knowing it unless it happened while they were standing still.

"If she swings back to the west," said Utah, "we'll be traveling southeast. We might wind up in a circle."

Stuart grinned. "You want to go back to Fort Union?"

Utah raised his voice. "I'd sure like to be there, but I'd rather go with that wind than against it."

Stuart divided the rest of the sack of corn among the mules. Tumbleweeds floated past occasionally, bounding over the prairie in long, rolling arcs.

Stuart examined the grass and tried to find a way to tell north from south, but failed.

"If there was trees," said Utah, "I could tell you—but here there ain't nothin'."

"We'll do the best we can. What's your position today?"

"Number three."

Stuart nodded. He faced into the wind. "Get 'em harnessed up!" he shouted.

Pablo was leading that day. He had trouble keeping the big mules down to a walk, for they were Missouri mules and twice the size of the little Mexican ones, but Pablo sawed at the reins and kept them down.

They stopped at noon, and Stuart let the mules graze. He hoped they would find water that night.

The men were silent as they crowded around the whipping fire. Stuart looked up from moving the coffee pot and almost butted Fisher under the chin with it. He caught Fisher looking to their rear. "Lost something?" he asked.

Fisher said, "I was tryin' to figure if that's west."

"If you find out," said Stuart, "tell me."

Utah said, "I think the wind is back in the west. It seemed to be bearin' to the left this morning."

Fisher looked up quickly. "It was bearin' to the right."

Utah's eyes narrowed. "You're crazy as a loon," he said.

Fisher glanced at him, stared for an instant, then suddenly leaped across the fire and grabbed Utah by the throat.

Stuart wheeled and stuck his six-shooter into Fisher's side. "Cut it out!" he commanded.

Fisher's arms dropped. He glared at Stuart. "If that old man ever says I'm crazy again—"

"You better leave that old man alone," said Stuart. "He's likely to slip into your bedroom some night with a knife. He's as good at that as any Indian."

"You take that gun out of my stomach and I'll knife-fight with him."

Stuart saw Pablo standing at Fisher's rear with his hand at his belt. Stuart shook his head, and Pablo's hand dropped slowly.

Stuart backed away and put his six-shooter in its holster. They were all within a few feet, watching him, and he said, talking loud against the wind, "We're lost and we don't know which way the wind is blowing. About all we can do is guess. But nobody's leaving the train. The man who leaves is a dead man. He wouldn't get more than twenty miles by himself." He looked at Fisher. "I know your nerves are raw, but that's no excuse for going to pieces like a bunch of women." He was deliberately haranguing them. "If we hang together, we're all right. We got food and water, and we'll be bound to wind up somewhere on the eastern Caprock."

"The wind might blow for weeks," said Brisket. "That means we'll get home before it quits."

Fisher said, "I don't aim to wander around up here until our water is gone."

Stuart said sharply, "You can take your share of the water and light out now—on foot."

"You're sentencin' me to death!" Fisher said hoarsely.

"Or you can stay here and drive your wagon like a man," said Stuart.

Fisher glared at him for a moment. Then he looked around at the others. And once again he seemed beaten down. "I'll drive my wagon," he said.

They found no water that day and made a second dry camp that night. Stuart fed the mules corn but gave them only a swallow of water apiece. One more day like this one could be serious.

The next morning the wind was blowing against the left front corner of the wagons, which had once again been left broadside to the wind. It was utterly hopeless to try to determine any direction, and Stuart ordered the course held with the wind quartering at their left rear.

Utah was number two that day, and he grinned when Stuart went by. "One thing for sure! Injuns have a hell of a time findin' us this kind of weather!"

Stuart realized that those words, even though they were spoken against the constant howl of wind and the incessant gritting of sand on the wagons, would carry downwind. He looked up and saw Fisher staring at them.

In early afternoon they came across a buffalo-wallow lake. The water was about a foot deep and the color of tea, but the mules were glad to drink it. The men got down on their knees, pushed their bandannas down into it to strain the bugs and pollywogs and drank all they could hold.

Stuart put the good water together in three barrels and filled the others from the wallow.

Dusty got up and wiped his mouth on his sleeve. He squeezed his bandanna dry. The water he squeezed out was caught by the wind and torn away without reaching the ground. "Mighty strong water," said Dusty, "but good and wet."

"Know what lake this is?" asked Utah.

Stuart shook his head. "Must be the only one for quite a spell, the way the critters are comin' to it."

Stuart nodded. Two mustangs, a small herd of antelope and a coyote were drinking at the same time. When animals get thirsty enough, they aren't fussy about their neighbors.

Regretfully, he shot one of the antelope with his six-shooter. The rest went on drinking. He pulled the carcass out, skinned it and wrapped the hams, loin and shoulders in the skin. He dropped the bundle in Utah's wagon. "We'll eat meat tonight," he said.

"We may have to eat it raw," said Utah. "You shoulda saved the liver."

They went on, Fisher leading out behind Stuart, who was on the gray. Stuart thought the wind was stronger than it had been the day before. And he knew it was changing, for, while they had been at the wallow, it had moved to their left again. The best they could do was keep running before it and hope the changes of direction would even up. He guessed they would if the train kept going long enough. The trouble was that the trip would be twice as long, and they might not get to water.

They camped that night under a shoulder-high cliff that nobody recognized. Below it was a sandy draw, and they got water by digging close to the west side just under the cliff. Watering the mules at the holes was a long and arduous job, for the water rose slowly, it was soon dark, and they could not make a fire big enough to provide light.

Stuart opened another sack of corn and gave the animals a good feed.

For a week now the wind had beaten at them, never letting up for a moment, never slackening its pressure, always tearing at them with its force, scouring them with the sand it carried.

"Them tumbleweeds now must come from Californy," said Utah.

"They'll wind up over in Indian Territory," said Brisket.

"Like hell!" said Utah. "The Tesecato Canyon will be full of them things when we get back."

The next day Utah was in first place. Stuart was hopeful they were getting somewhere near the Caprock, but Utah said they had gone too far south and were somewhere in the middle of the southern Llano.

That night they found a small lake—not a wallow—loaded with alkali. Stuart held the mules back from it and put enough in a bucket for a swallow. The mules would not drink it anyway, so he knew it was very bad. A couple of cow skeletons around the edges, patches of hide still sticking to the dry ribs, showed that the mules' judgment was good. A cow would drink anything, but a mule was usually pretty smart about water.

"We better not use it," Stuart said, sitting down. "We

39

don't want any sick men on our hands. We got enough trouble the way it is."

Utah tasted it and made a face. "Where do you reckon we are now?" he asked.

Stuart shrugged, then raised his eyebrows. "What are you grinning about?"

Utah's leathery old face was crinkled up. "I'm thinkin' about them Indians tryin' to trail us. They're sure gittin' their money's worth."

"You think they are behind us?"

"That dun mule's ears was twitchin' all day."

Stuart stared. "You never told me."

"They wasn't close enough."

"Could you tell what tribe it was?" Stuart asked jokingly.

Utah stared reproachfully at him. "You'll think I'm lyin'," he said, "but the tribe is Cheyenne."

Stuart gave that a good thought. If the Indians were following them and had any luck, they'd probably catch up to the train tomorrow. The fact they were still following indicated that the train was doing pretty well even with the never-ceasing wind. It also indicated they were after the powder and lead, for it was not like Indians to trail anybody in such weather.

They had drawn the wagons in on what Stuart supposed was the east side, set them broadside to the wind again, stretched the canvas and built a small fire. The antelope meat had helped him to stretch out their food supply, but that would be running out in a day or two.

There were no wild animals around this lake—which verified the mules' judgment and also failed to bring any game within gunshot. They used the last of the cornmeal and made coffee.

Fisher said sourly, "Damn' poor grub."

Stuart said evenly, "It may get worse."

"Anybody know where we are?" Fisher demanded.

Nobody answered. Stuart said, "You ought to know as well as any of us."

"Meaning what?" Fisher was edgy.

"Meaning nothing except that you've been over the plains a lot."

Fisher slung the coffee grounds out of his tin cup and poured more coffee out of the pot. "It looks like the south plains to me—but exactly where, I don't know."

Stuart nodded.

Pablo said, "I've seen these salt lakes when I—"

"Shut up!" Fisher said explosively.

"Stop it!" Stuart said.

Fisher glowered at him, and Stuart waited for Fisher to jump him. Then Fisher grimaced and held the cup to his lips.

Brisket said contemplatively, "Fisher, you been wantin' to take Pablo into camp for a long time. Would I do instead?"

Stuart said sharply, "Sit down, Brisket!" His voice rose above the screaming wind. "Save your fighting till we get home!"

Utah said sourly, "We're savin' an awful lot."

"It'll keep," said Stuart.

He and Utah made a careful inspection of the wagons before they went to bed. The wind was still rising, and the steady push of it sometimes made the wagon boxes move. Utah's wagon was on the apex at the left. Brisket had pulled into the front spot, since he would lead out tomorrow. They examined the ropes and the canvas and saw that all were well fastened.

"Them axles will need more grease before long," said Utah.

"We'll know it in plenty of time. We'll hear them screeching."

"We could as well grease 'em now."

Stuart decided against it. Men could endure a lot, but they had limits. Greasing the axles in that wind might be the limit, for it was physically exhausting just to be in the wind all day. A man's nerves got ground pretty thin from the constant pressure and the scouring of the sand.

Utah got Stuart off to one side. "Maybe we better sleep out a ways tonight—if that mule's ears was gittin' the right message."

Stuart thought about it. "The best thing for them would be to stampede the *mulada*. Then they'd have it all to themselves."

"Unless they wanted the mules to pull the wagons."

Stuart looked at him. "They're fighting a war. They might want the mules, too."

"They'll need everything they can get."

"We'll hobble and picket the mules," Stuart said, "right in front of the wagons. You and I will go out about a hundred yards."

41

Utah said, "I ain't so sure it's smart. Them Comanches are the worst Indians in the West for slippin' into camp at night. They can take off your boots without you knowin' it."

Stuart looked at him. "The mule's ears said they were Cheyenne," he noted.

Utah nodded slowly. "You're darin' me to bet my scalp on a mule's ears. All right—but I ain't aimin' to sleep much."

"Neither am I."

Fisher looked at them curiously when they took their beds away from the lee of the wagons, but they did not explain. Stuart lay down with his boots on and his six-shooter just under the blanket. He didn't dare put his head under the blanket, but lay facing away from the wagons, hoping that even a Comanche would not hear or see everything in that wind.

He slept only in snatches, and, after a very long time, he felt sure it was getting near morning, so he went back to the wagons and set to work to build a fire to make coffee. He woke Pablo and set him to keep an eye on the south, with his rifle in his hands. "And don't stand out in the open," Stuart told him. "Stay alongside a wagon. Indians are trailing us."

Stuart saw Utah on his feet and motioned him in. It was beginning to get light.

"They should have attacked by now if they're going to," said Brisket.

"They would have had to wait till morning to follow us. Not even a Comanche could follow that trail at night."

"I'll just stand in between the wheels," said Utah. "If any comes, maybe I'll see him first."

"Your wagon will be in the rear today," said Stuart. "I think I'd better lead the gray and ride your wagon facing the wind."

"She'll grind your eyelids off."

Stuart took Dusty and Fisher with him to get the mules. They brought them in and harnessed up. They put the extra mules on the lead line, and Stuart tied it to the number two wagon to keep the mules away from the lake.

He went back to the fire.

"I vote we turn back to the right today," said Fisher.

Stuart said to him, "Nobody asked you to vote. You'll go along with the rest of us."

Fisher started to smile sardonically but didn't finish it.

A sharp crack from Utah's Henry carbine and a dull crash from Pablo's six-shooter sent them diving for cover. Utah shouted, "Here they come!"

Pablo screamed something Stuart didn't hear. Then the Indians, half-naked and feathered, swept around them in a wheeling circle.

They had been silent until the rifle spoke. Then they started their age-old war cry.

Stuart dived between the wagons with Utah. Pablo backed up to meet them.

"Come in here together!" Stuart told them.

Brisket and Dusty and Fisher crawled under the first row of wagons and joined them. The six men were then concentrated between Utah's single wagon and the next two. Beyond them were the second two, for breastworks; behind Utah's wagon was the lake.

The Indians were still sounding their war cry. It came and went eerily on the wind. Arrows thudded into the wagons until the first two wagons bristled.

"There's sixty Cheyennes," Utah noted. "That mule knew what he was talkin' about."

The Indians were not shooting bullets, which meant they were indeed out of ammunition, for in that place and with that wind there was no danger of shots calling for help. There could be no doubt that the Indians were after the ammunition.

Stuart squatting between the wagons, tried to figure out what would happen next. They could easily stand off the Indians all day, for it would not be too difficult to crawl into the wagons and get their weapons and boxes of cartridges. The thought struck him that it was strange to be shooting store-bought cartridges to protect powder and lead that the Army would hand-load. But then, the Army hadn't adopted breech-loaders until the Civil War was practically over.

Utah said, "Damn, I wish you'd brought the coffee."

Stuart said, "It wasn't ready."

"It will be before we get out of here."

Stuart fired his rifle at a redskin who was sweeping in close, but he missed. The Cheyenne dropped over on the side of his paint horse and swept by the wagons. Stuart stood up to try for the horse, but an arrow from under the horse's neck zipped past his ear and sped into the lake behind him.

Utah shouted, "Git down, you idjit!"

43

Stuart got down. The Cheyenne went by three times in a hard gallop, and at first Stuart figured he was making medicine, but the third time he saw the reason. The Cheyenne had a knife in his teeth, and he was slashing at the lead line for the extra mules every time he went by. The third time he cut it in two, and the mules, excited by the yelling, shooting and powder smoke, stampeded off toward the south.

Stuart groaned. The Cheyennes had outguessed them.

"There wasn't nothin' you could do anyways," Utah said, shouting against the wind.

The Cheyennes drew off and divided into two parties. One went around the lake and began its wheeling charge from the rear of the wagons. The other stayed in front and began an identical charge at the same time.

"Smart Injuns!" said Utah. "They're learnin' fast!"

"Too damn fast!" said Stuart, firing.

An Indian dropped, but the wheeling circle drew closer. And now there were only three men to face the charge from each direction.

At that moment, Utah, who was near the front of the wagon in the second column, groaned and said, "Oh, the red-skinned bastards!"

"You hit?" asked Stuart.

"Not yet I ain't—but they're takin' the first wagon!"

Stuart stood up for an instant. Arrows flew around him so thickly he did not even have time for a shot, but he saw three Cheyennes in moccasins and breechclouts leap onto the wagon seat from the east. He tried to stand up again for a shot at them, but the Cheyennes were keeping him down with arrows.

"They learned that from Colonel Miles!" Utah said.

"That wagon has the powder in it!" said Stuart.

"It's no good to us now," said Brisket.

Dusty was working his lever-action rifle on the other side, and suddenly there were two Indians in the dirt.

Stuart stayed down. He heard the Indians yell as they drove the wagon away, mules at a gallop.

He stared at a big X daubed on the tailgate in clay.

CHAPTER VI

THE wagon went out of sight in the sand-laden wind. The Indians on both sides of them pulled back until they were almost invisible in the storm. Stuart saw one vague shape detach itself from the north side and ride after the wagon. A moment later the Indian was back, and the party went into a huddle.

"They'll be comin' after the lead," said Utah.

Stuart turned to look at Fisher and saw the man's hard face suddenly contorted with something like consternation. Fisher started to stand up, but Stuart swung his rifle on him and said, "Keep down."

Fisher glared at him and slowly got back under cover.

Stuart went around to the back end of Utah's wagon and found an X drawn with clay. He looked Fisher in the eye and said levelly, "When I find out for sure who did that, I'm going to fill him so full of lead they won't be able to lift him on a flatcar with a block and tackle."

Fisher said, "Don't look at me. There's five more men here, including yourself. It looks to me like you're as good a suspect as any."

Stuart said harshly, "Brisket will drive your wagon. You'll walk."

Fisher, his eyes ominous under the flopping brim of his hat, asked, "You tryin' to force a showdown, Nichols?"

Stuart said, "Whenever you're ready."

Fisher faced Stuart, wetting his lips, and looked around him. "Your men would shoot me down," he said.

"They probably would," said Stuart. From the corner of one eye he saw Dusty moving in behind Fisher.

Fisher stared at him for an instant. He swallowed, and the red whiskers moved on his weathered neck. "You've got me five against one," he said.

Stuart said, "It's a damn' good thing, the way I figure it."

"I didn't have nothin' to do with it," said Fisher.

"You're a liar by the clock."

Fisher said doggedly, "You're puttin' the blame on the wrong man, Nichols. You could be mistaken."

Stuart said, "The outside chance that I'm wrong is all that's saving your life." He motioned to Dusty, who took Fisher's six-shooter.

Stuart said, "You use some of that alkali water to wash that X off of Utah's wagon, and then you use some of that mud to put an X on Dusty's wagon. If the Cheyennes come back, we won't make it easy for them." He looked at Fisher coldly. "Too bad you didn't know the stuff would be in separate wagons when you rode out northeast from Union. Then you could have told them to look for two wagons."

As they were cutting an arrow out of a mule's rump and daubing the wound with axle grease, Utah said in a low voice, "You shoulda had it out with him."

Stuart put the lid back on the can of axle grease. "I'm not as sure of these things as I was five years ago. In eighteen-seventy, if I had caught a man doing what Fisher has done, I'd have shot him without a second thought. Now I keep thinking, 'What if I was wrong?' "

Utah nodded. "When you start thinkin' things like that, you're through on the frontier."

"Didn't *you* ever have doubts?"

"Sure," said Utah. "That's when I quit living with the Indians. They don't change. They grow up to know it's kill or be killed, and they never forget it till they die. A white man has got no business around them when he begins to doubt."

"I daresay you'd shoot to kill if an Indian came at you, and you'd lift his hair afterward."

"Sure," said Utah. "You never change over completely— not unless you're funny in the head. You begin to doubt when you're sitting around quiet. But when you're in the middle of things you act like you always did."

Stuart pulled his hat down tighter against the wind.

46

"We're harnessed up. We'd better move."

Brisket was shouting against the wind. "The pesky Injuns turned over the coffee pot!"

They pulled out. Figuring that the lake was to the south of where they wanted to go, Stuart headed to what he thought was northeast, with the wind quartering at their left rear. He cut farther east than he thought the Cheyennes had gone, to avoid running into them if they should return.

Stuart, riding ahead, watched Fisher walking with his back to the wind. Come to think of it, he thought now, most of the Indian arrows had either gone high over their heads or low into the wagon beds. It seemed obvious that the Indians had been trying to avoid killing somebody, though he'd never thought an Indian would pay that much attention to the life of a white man.

They found no water that day, and camped on the open prairie. The never-easing pressure of the wind was so a part of them now a man felt like cursing it directly.

They used more water from the kegs that night, and, although the mules were watered meagerly, there were only two kegs of water left. Stuart had them all fill their canteens and told them not to touch the canteens unless they found themselves in an emergency. He looked at the little group around him. It was now a question of survival, and he felt responsible for them all. But in the face of that relentless wind, he did not have much encouragement to offer them. "We'll keep going," he said. "We're bound to get to the Caprock sometime."

But the next day the mules began to balk, and that afternoon they covered not over a mile or two. Stuart gave out water rations to the men. He didn't water the mules because it wouldn't do any good. They had already had too much of the wind.

The mule with the injured hip did not get up that morning, and Stuart shot it with his pistol. They were short a mule on Utah's wagon—the one containing the lead. They took out the straightener for Utah's lead pair and fastened the singletree directly to the chain. Utah said, "Hell, it don't make no difference to a mule this kind of weather how much he's pullin'."

But it did. The added weight told on the other mules, and by noon they were balking again. Stuart figured they had covered about six miles that morning. And for nine straight days now, the wind had not let up for even a moment.

They made a dry camp at noon. Utah said, "The wind's been shiftin' all day."

Stuart nodded. "Your wheel horse is lame."

"That lead makes a heavy load."

"I'll move a mule from Brisket's team."

They harnessed up about two o'clock and went on. The lame mule balked an hour later. The train was held up most of the afternoon. They tried everything, even to filling its ear with gravel and tying it down against its head, but the mule finally lay down in the harness and refused to get up.

They cut it out of the team, and that left Brisket with four mules.

There was a sack of shelled corn left, but Stuart did not feed it to them. It would only make their thirst worse.

The train started up again, but two mules—one of Dusty's and one of Utah's—refused to move.

Utah said, "We better hit water tonight."

They turned the lame mule loose and watched to see if it would head for water, but it didn't. It fell in behind the wagons.

Pablo shook his head at that. "Water's *muy allá*—very far," he said.

They made two miles more that afternoon, but were finally forced to stop. The wind was rising again in force. Stuart pulled the wagons into a shallow draw and started the men to making a fire, while he rode the gray down the draw to see if it might lead to water.

Apparently it did not, though he discovered a growth of mesquite at one point that indicated there was water somewhere beneath. "Somewhere beneath" might mean fifty feet, but he went back to the wagons and got Pablo and two shovels. They dug down ten feet without finding moisture. Stuart followed the draw on down until dark, but the draw got no bigger and finally got smaller and apparently closed up again. Probably there was a spring at the higher end during wet weather, but there wasn't anything damp there now.

He rode back to camp in the dark, the wind tearing at his clothes, the sand beating at his face. Now even his hands were getting sore where the sand had scoured his skin for so many days.

He could not see the fire over a hundred yards away because of the sand. He went in to find them all huddled around it.

Utah looked up. "Half of them mules won't get up in the morning," he said.

Stuart dismounted and tied the gray to a wagon wheel. "I'm afraid you're right."

"We better make up our minds what we're going to leave behind."

Fisher spoke up. "We better leave the wagons and ride the mules as far as they will go."

"That wouldn't be far," said Stuart.

Brisket asked, "How much farther to go, Stuart?"

Stuart squatted before the struggling fire. "Maybe ten miles—maybe a hundred."

Dusty said, against the wind, "It'd be a shame to leave the wagons if we was close."

"On the other hand," said Stuart, "we're out of water. We have about a gallon apiece for each man. Suppose we try to drive the mules on and spend all day tomorrow to make five or six miles. By that time we'll be shorter on water, and maybe still a week away from the Caprock."

Brisket asked, "Are you figurin' we better abandon the wagons?"

Stuart glanced at him. "It works out that way."

"But—"

"If we leave the wagons behind and turn the mules loose, we might make it to the Caprock in three days. And if the wind goes down, we'll be able to see the sun and find out where we are."

Pablo said, "The sun—she's gone a long time."

"What if we don't make it in three days?" asked Dusty.

Stuart shrugged. "Maybe we can make it in four."

"As long as the water holds out."

They were silent for a few moments. Utah said, "We ought to be able to find the wagons later on."

"We can leave the wagons as they stand," Stuart said, "except for one thing."

"What's that?" asked Dusty.

"A ton of lead is in Utah's wagon. The Cheyennes have already got the powder, and, if they get the lead, too, the war on the Llano may go on indefinitely. A lot of soldiers will be killed."

Brisket said, "You think the Indians might win?"

Stuart glanced up quickly at Fisher and saw a strange light in the unshaven man's eyes. "It's possible," Stuart said.

Utah observed, "You figgered out somethin'."

"I think so."

"Whatever it is, we better get at it. I'm tired of bein' lost."

Stuart looked at the red-eyed men around him. The strain of the incessant, driving wind was showing in their gaunt faces, in the skin stretched tightly over their cheekbones.

"We'll cache the lead," he said.

He looked up again at Fisher and surprised a calculating look in Fisher's watery blue eyes.

"We'll cache it," Stuart said, "so it'll be hard to find. And, if the Indians do find it, they won't be able to use it for quite a while. We'll melt it down," he went on, "and pour it in one big hole. It'll be one solid chunk, and it will take the Indians at least a week to figure out how to get it out after they find it. They haven't got power enough to lift a one-ton piece of lead, and they haven't got hacksaws."

"They could build a big fire and melt it down," said Brisket.

"A fire like that could be seen for miles. And by the time they find it, the Army will have patrols up here."

There was silence for a moment as each man thought it over.

"It sure will be a big chunk of lead," said Utah finally.

CHAPTER VII

STUART said, "About half a mile that way—" He pointed—"is plenty of mesquite. That'll burn long and hot. Three of you can take turns on the grubbing hoes. The others will dig a hole and get the brass kettles ready."

"We'll be up all night," said Fisher.

"I expect we will."

"Anyway," Fisher said, "you can't melt it all at once. One kettleful won't stick to what's already in the hole."

"It sure will," said Stuart. "The hot metal will melt the other where it hits, and it will stick together pretty tight. After a kettleful or two, the metal in the hole will retain a lot of heat. They might be able to pry off a couple of chunks with a crowbar," he conceded. "But the Indians haven't got crowbars yet."

"Maybe," said Utah, "some whites will start selling crowbars as soon as this gets around."

Fisher swung to him angrily, but Utah stood with his hand on his six-shooter, and Fisher controlled himself.

Brisket emptied his coffee cup. He got up and went over to the nearest wagon and tied the cup to it with a rawhide thong. The wind caught the cup and blew it out straight, then banged it against the wagon and threw it out again. "I'll take a grubbing hoe," he said.

"It's already dark," Stuart pointed out. "You'll have to work by feel."

"That's nothin' new," said Brisket.

Pablo and Dusty got up to go with him.

51

"Don't go any farther than you have to," said Stuart. "If you get lost, follow the draw."

He dug a hole as big as a washtub for the fire, and got the first handful of brush in it. He set the kettles deep in the coals, and Utah opened up the canvas and began to unload the heavy bars of lead.

Fisher dug at the big hole in silence, throwing the dirt to the wind, which constantly swept it away and out of sight.

Brisket came up with an armful of mesquite roots. Stuart arranged them around the kettles.

"She meltin' yet?" asked Utah.

"Not yet but soon," said Stuart.

Within another hour the kettle was half full of melted lead—about all he could lift, Stuart figured. He put on his gloves and padded the bail with a piece of canvas and carried it ten feet. He tipped the kettle with a stick of mesquite and poured the silvery metal into the hole.

He kept them at it most of the night, bucketful after bucketful, and finally all of the bars were melted down and the hole was fairly well-filled with one solid mass of lead. It wasn't a very big hole, really, for the bulk of the lead was less than its weight would indicate. As each new half kettleful had been poured, it had welded itself to the mass, and now, with 2,200 pounds of lead in the cache, the heat from the big lump was terrific.

Utah helped him cover the lead. They were careful not to dig up grass and not to change the looks of the surface by digging too deep. "In a couple of hours," Stuart said, "the wind will smooth it down until even a Comanche will have trouble finding it."

Utah said, "It looks to me like there's somethin' you didn't think about."

"What? The wagons?"

"You thought about 'em, then?"

Stuart scratched his whiskered chin. "We can get maybe five to ten miles from here before the mules play out entirely. When they do, we'll leave the wagons and go on."

"They'll still find the wagons."

"And that will mean the lead is somewhere within a ten-mile radius, because I'm going to change course in every direction. When we get through, the wagons may be pointed at the lead instead of away from it."

Utah nodded. He was still hatless. "This wind tears up

52

everything," he conceded. "There's not even droppings to show where the mules spent the night. There's nothin' stays put but bear grass."

Stuart went back to the fire. "You can all go to bed now for a couple of hours. I'll put some coffee in the coals." He looked at them—Utah, Brisket, Pablo, Dusty, Fisher. Their faces were drawn tautly now, and the creases in their skin were filled with dirt. The glow of the firelight slanting upward gave them strange, eerie expressions. "I just wanted to say," he told them, "that if any man is caught marking this spot he will be shot on sight."

Fisher worked his mouth a moment. "The lead is government property," he said. "Don't you aim for the Army to find it?"

Stuart said coldly, "That's my lookout. Yours is not to try anything." He went on in a cold voice: "You set the Indians after us, Fisher, and I'm going to see that you answer for it."

Fisher looked at Stuart from under the big hat. "Someday you'll eat them words," he said.

Stuart stared challengingly at him. "Now?" he asked.

For a moment he thought Fisher would take it up. The man glared at him, and slow hatred formed in his buttermilk-blue eyes—a hatred intensified by the indignity Stuart was now forcing on him. He looked around at the other four but saw no sympathy. He turned back to Stuart. "This is no time to fight," he said in a surly voice. "We got enough trouble."

Stuart relaxed.

He got a couple of hours' sleep after he heard Fisher's deep snore. Then it was light again—a weird half light that filtered through the driving sand—and he rolled to his feet and pulled on his boots. Utah came up, bent against the wind. "We lost a passenger," he said, dropping to the ground.

"Fisher?"

"He took your horse too."

Stuart swore. "If he mistreats that horse, I won't have any compunctions in dealing with him."

Utah nodded. "I couldn't tell how long he'd been gone," he said. "Too much wind."

Stuart stood up, partially shielded from the wind by the nearest wagon.

"You're goin' to have some things to settle when you get

53

back home," said Utah. "You got a neighbor that set the Indians on us, that stole a horse. He looks like to me like he's worked out on a mighty small limb."

"I could have killed him," Stuart said, pouring coffee.

"But you went soft."

"Well, I don't kill a white man as quick as I used to."

Four of the twenty mules did not get up. They were six short. Fourteen mules for four wagons.

Since one wagon was empty, they redistributed the loads and started out. The mules looked bad; their ribs showed through their hides as if they hadn't eaten for a month.

They made fair time that morning and stopped at noon. With the wind and the sand and the half light, they might well have been where they were the first day on the Llano.

Utah, chewing a slice of half-fried bacon, asked, "You mark that cache?"

"Sure I did."

"I suppose Fisher did, too, before he left."

"Yes, he dug a hole off to one side and buried a grubbing hoe in it, with the handle sticking out about a foot." He sipped the coffee. "I took the grubbing hoe out and put it back in the wagon." He added with assurance, "Fisher will get what's coming to him sooner or later."

Utah looked at him. "Unless the Indians win."

Stuart, startled, thought about it. Finally he nodded. "The Indians have to win for him to make anything. I guess then he figures he'll be able to take the Tesecato over all by himself, because the Schoolers and the Nichols will be either run off or massacred."

"Yeah," said Dusty. "You remember how he complained about how dry it was down at his place and how nice things looked on the Rocking Seven?"

Pablo nodded with assurance. "He's hungry man. He wants —many things."

"And figures to get them if the Indians conquer the Panhandle," said Stuart.

"They can't win, can they?" asked Brisket.

Stuart said slowly, "Some people think they could."

Three mules failed to get up after they ate. Two more balked in the harness. Stuart said, "I guess this is as far as the wagons go."

They unhitched the mules and let them go in the driving

54

wind. There was half a canteenful of water for each man. Stuart said, "We'd better take the bacon with us."

They got the tow-sacks that had held the corn and packed a small amount of food in them. Stuart warned them to take as little as possible, for the food would not be any good unless they found water. They took one blanket apiece, and Stuart took a grubbing hoe.

By that time, the mules had disappeared. Utah had watched carefully, but they had gone in all directions. "I don't reckon one of them smelled water," he said. "Most of them drifted into the wind."

They walked all afternoon, partially propelled by the wind. That night they had one swallow of water apiece and no coffee. Stuart said, "We must have covered eleven or twelve miles this afternoon. The Llano can't last forever."

Utah said, "I ain't so sure."

"Forever is a long time," said Pablo.

Stuart looked at the men around him. They had lost fifteen or twenty pounds apiece, and their whiskered faces looked haggard, their cheeks hollow, their lips black. He knew what it was—the eternal wind seemed to suck the last drop of moisture out of a man's body. Their condition was intensified by the awful feeling of being lost in the middle of an endless wilderness of wind and sand and half light that would never end. Stuart watched them carefully. The first to crack, he thought, would be Dusty.

They walked on that night, going with the wind, for there was nothing else to guide them. The Llano was a vast dark bowl with sides that extended to the sky, and inside it they were being hammered and torn by the unceasing wind.

They slept for four hours and then went on. Stuart was not sure, but he suspected the others might have finished their water by that time. He saved his last mouthful.

They started again when the darkness lifted. The temperature rose, and they went forward interminably into the swirling sand. It began to seem to Stuart as though the sheets of wind-driven sand were hypnotizing him. He was suddenly brought out of his half trance by a voice at his shoulder: "I want my pay!"

He turned to stare at Brisket. Pablo, who had been ahead, came back. Utah and Dusty closed in silently.

"My pay!" Brisket shouted. "I'm goin' to town! I want my pay!"

55

Stuart looked at Brisket, saw the wild light in his blood-shot eyes. "We're all going in tomorrow," he said placatingly.

"I don't wanta wait till tomorrow. I want my pay now. I promised that girl at the Cottonwood Saloon I'd buy her a drink. I want my pay!"

"I'll get it," said Stuart, and took hold of the grubbing hoe slung over his shoulder. He laid his tow-sack on the ground and slid the grubbing hoe out of its rawhide sling. He took hold of the handle near the metal, straightened up suddenly and cracked Brisket over the top of the head.

He watched Brisket fold up. "We may have to tie his hands when he comes to," he said.

They waited, watchful. Presently Brisket stirred, and then sat up, rubbing his head. "Somebody hit me?" he asked.

"You fell," Stuart said, watching him.

Brisket drew a deep breath and got to his feet. Suddenly he struck at Stuart and began to shout hoarsely. "You did it! You don't want to give me my pay! You held back on me! You did it before! You no-good, cheatin', Texas pig-driver!"

Stuart frowned. Dusty and Utah closed in on Brisket, but he got up and threw them off like dead leaves from a cotton-wood tree. Pablo and Stuart moved in silently. They finally got Brisket down by their weight, tied his hands behind him and made him walk ahead.

Utah said, "He's in bad shape."

Stuart, weak from the exertion, nodded. "By tomorrow he won't be able to walk."

Late that afternoon, plodding with the wind because there was nothing else to do, they sat down to talk it over. Brisket was voiceless, having screamed himself hoarse. Dusty said, "How much further can we go, Mr. Nichols?"

Stuart shook his head. "I don't know. We'll keep each other going as long as we can." He looked up at the sky without hope. "We ought to be getting somewhere."

Pablo seemed to be standing it better than any of them. His face was gaunt and shrunken, but there did not seem to be much difference in his voice or his actions.

Utah said, "I'm getting mighty tired, Stuart. Maybe I better rest a while and you fellers go on and see if you can find anything."

"No, we'll stick together," said Stuart.

Pablo said, "I help, *Señor Utah*."

Stuart said, "You've got your hands full with Brisket."

Pablo shook his head. *"Señor Brisket,* he won't live tomorrow this time."

Stuart staggered up with his tow-sack on his shoulder. "Let's move on a ways. It isn't dark yet."

They got up slowly. Pablo was walking with Brisket, talking to him.

It was like walking in a dream—a nightmare of sand that traveled in horizontal sheets, that had scoured the backs of their hands until they were bleeding, that beat at their hats and clothing until the sound of it became a torment to their ears.

And then, just before dark, Pablo shouted: *"Señor! Señor! Señor! La Ceja!* The Caprock!"

Stuart stumbled forward and stared, leaning back against the wind to avoid being blown over the edge. Utah staggered up beside him. "I thought maybe the God-damn' thing had been filled up by this time," he said in a cracked voice.

CHAPTER VIII

THEY camped on a ledge just under the top that night. Stuart gave his last water to Brisket, and for the first time they were relieved of the pressure of the wind, though it howled and screamed above them and the sand drifted over the edge of the Caprock in a sheet like a fine waterfall.

Eventually they went to sleep, exhausted, and a long time later Stuart awoke with the sun in his face.

At first he did not realize what it was, and he thought for a moment he, like Brisket, had lost his head.

He sat up and saw the sun was shining. Fine sand lay in the wrinkles of his clothing, but it was no longer sifting down over the edge of the Caprock just above them.

Brisket yawned and opened his eyes. He had lost a great deal of weight, and his eyes were sunken in his head. He squinted at the sun and looked around him. He looked at Stuart and then down at the 500-foot cliff below him, and he drew back with a start. "How'd we git here?" he asked, perplexed.

Stuart said, through cracked lips, "We walked."

Utah shook his head and sat up slowly. He was about all in, thought Stuart. This was no trip for a man of his age. "I ain't been so glad to see the sun since I was snowed in one winter on top of the Sangre de Cristo," Utah said feebly.

Dusty, drawn and shrunken, grinned. "The sun is sure nice," he said.

Pablo, a little gray and showing the strain in the tightness of the skin over his high cheekbones, nevertheless looked

58

relieved and optimistic. "Maybe I go back to Fort Union some day after all," he said.

They got back on top of the Llano. They had no water, but down below, in the bottom of the canyon, a silvery stream ran quietly through green meadows.

Stuart pointed. "I think that's the Quitaque. What do you say, Pablo?"

Pablo nodded solemnly. "*Sí*, this is the Quitaque, and there is a *puerta* not far from here—an old *comanchero* trail."

"You go north," Stuart said, "and I'll go south. We ought to hit it within a couple of miles."

Half an hour later, he heard Pablo's high, singing voice: "*Aquí, aquí! Vengan aquí.*"

It made him feel so good he was weak in the knees for a moment. Then he got his strength under him and began walking back. He saw the other three ahead of him. They waited at the trail until he caught up, then all went down.

They stumbled down the steep trail, diagonally across the face of the vertical cliff. They reached the bottom and spread out in a ragged line. They were weak but held up by the sure knowledge of water. Stuart forced himself to get ahead.

With a sudden surge of strength they ran the last two hundred yards, but Stuart warned them. "Don't do more than rinse out your mouth or you'll be sick," he said. "Take off your boots and sit with your feet in the water."

Brisket could not hold himself back. He rushed in up to his knees and fell at full length. Stuart and Pablo pulled him out to keep him from drowning. . . .

They borrowed some horses from the Toadfrog spread and dropped down onto the Bar M shortly after noon. Anne Schooler came out of the door to meet them, and stood staring as if she couldn't believe her eyes.

"Stuart Nichols, what *happened* to you?"

He pulled his horse to a stop. "Like you know, we went to Fort Union with a wagon train, and the storm caught us on the way back."

"You look terrible," she said in a low voice filled with sympathy.

Stuart dismounted. "We'll take a little time out." He tied the reins to the peeled cottonwood pole that served as a hitch-rail. "We won't stay long, ma'am." He remembered the proprieties. "Where's Will?"

Anne held the door open for them. "He's down in the meadow trying to cut that hay."

"That should have been cut two weeks ago."

"He just didn't get at it. Will is always that way, you know." She bustled around the stove. "He feels pretty bad about it himself sometimes. He says if he could just once do something really worth-while he'd die happy!" She laughed —unnecessarily, Stuart thought. "I'm glad he didn't go with you. I would have been worried to death with him up there in that storm."

"It gets monotonous," Stuart observed, helping himself to the sugar.

Dusty said seriously, "It wouldn't be so bad monotonous, only it's always the same."

Anne sat down exactly as Stuart had expected her to, across the table from him. "Did you have trouble finding water?"

Brisket said, "It was right scarce, ma'am."

Stuart stole a look at her over his cup. She was right beautiful, he thought. He pushed the cup back and got up. "We'll be on our way, ma'am. Thank you kindly, and thank your husband for us."

They rode on to the Rocking Seven at a brisk trot, and, when they entered the high mesquite, Stuart saw his father go out into the yard on his crutches and stand there, staring at them. The cook came out and joined him, and Stuart took off his hat and waved.

George waved back, and sat on a stump, waiting for them.

"We're sure glad to see you," he said as they rode up.

Stuart grinned. "That's just the way *we* feel."

The rode to the corral, and Stuart stared at the far pen. "How'd the gray get here?"

"Fisher rode in yesterday from the north. Said he got separated from you."

Stuart looked at the gray and then at his father. "Was the gray treated all right?"

"I didn't see no sign of mistreatment," said George.

"It's a good thing for him."

George said thoughtfully, "It was funny he ended up with the only horse."

Stuart dismounted. "Not funny if you know Fisher as well as I do now."

"You could have charged him with horse-stealing if he hadn't brought the gray back home."

Stuart got down. "See that Slim takes these horses home tomorrow, will you, dad?"

Utah said, "Tell him not to ride this bay. It's like goin' over the rocks at the bottom of hell in a hay wagon."

CHAPTER IX

STUART and Utah, pretty well recovered after eating and sleeping intermittently all night, left early the next morning for Fort Sill to report to Whitehead. It took four days of hard riding.

Whitehead welcomed them with cigars. Stuart lit his, but Utah preferred a chew.

"Since you came in late," said Whitehead, "you must have had trouble."

Stuart told him about it, and Whitehead paced the floor. "The lead is buried in one piece. That was smart thinking, Mr. Nichols."

Stuart puffed hard on his cigar.

"Who set the Indians on you?"

Stuart told him all that had happened. "Maybe you better pick up Fisher and ask him some questions," he suggested.

Whitehead looked thoughtfully at him. "You say he owns the LHJ?"

"Supposedly."

"Then he isn't going to run away. He may be worth more to us if we watch him for a while."

Stuart made a sour face. "I should have shot him when I had an excuse."

"To recover your wagons and the supplies in them, and particularly the lead which you so ingeniously buried, I think you'd better see Colonel Miles. He's in the field about sixty miles north or northeast of your ranch."

"Give me four men and I'll start back from here."

"I can't spare four men. If the Cheyennes under Stone

Calf should win a victory over our forces, the Indians around Fort Sill would rebel overnight. Every available man is in the field at this moment.

"I will give you a letter to Miles; I can assure you he is anxious enough for that lead to provide a detail for you."

"How about horses?" asked Stuart.

"We do have remounts."

"I think we'll go by the ranch and get the men who were with me," said Stuart. "That Llano looks all alike when the sun is shining, but in a sandstorm—"

"It makes you feel like a hoot owl in a prairie-dog hole at midnight," said Utah.

Stuart got up. "I'd like to run into that bunch of Indians with a squad of cavalrymen. I think we could leave some dead Indians on the plains."

Whitehead looked at him curiously. "Mr. Nichols, once before I heard you express your bitterness toward Indians."

"Do you like 'em?" Stuart demanded.

Whitehead shrugged. "I don't seem to have that personal hatred for them that I detect in you. Is there some reason—"

Stuart took the cigar out of his mouth. "There's plenty of reason, Major. As a kid I was raised on the frontier, and I saw farmers' cabins after the Comanches had come and gone and left mutilated bodies all over the cleared grounds. I went searching for kids whose parents sent them into the brush before they themselves were tomahawked, and I found them with their brains knocked out against a tree. I was living with my parents on the Brazos when the Kiowas under White Horse raided down through there. I saw Mrs. Sherman after they raped her thirteen times and left her pinned to the floor with an arrow through both breasts. I watched her baby be born dead the next day, and I helped to bury Mrs. Sherman the day after." He stopped to stare through the window. "If I had my way, Major, I'd shoot every red-skinned bastard in the Southwest."

The major drew a deep breath and was silent for a moment. Then he said, "I'll show you how to find Miles." He pointed to a map on his desk. "Now here is the Salt Fork of Red River, and this is Whitefish Creek. We are quite sure that the Indians —perhaps in a number of groups—are scattered through these deep canyons north of the Red River. Miles is right in here at the moment. I suggest you study that map and familiarize yourself with it."

Stuart said, "Utah, you better memorize this."

Utah looked at the big map. "Miles is here?" he asked.

"Near there, at least."

"Two or three hundred men?"

"Yes."

"We'll find him."

"You must remember that this is all Indian country. There are small parties of Indians holed up all over the area. They offer no threat to an armed patrol, but they might attack two men." He smiled. "So I have given orders that you be mounted on the Army's best horses."

Utah grunted.

Stuart said, "I wish I knew for sure where Fisher went when he left us. He could have gone straight home, of course. A lone man traveling horseback and knowing where he was going—" He swung on Utah—"He should made made it long before he did. He was only a day ahead of us, and we were on foot."

"I thought of that," said Utah.

Whitehead was pouring from a bottle into three glasses. "Aside from any purely mercenary aspect," he said, handing a glass to each of them, "I think your very great perseverance under considerable handicaps deserves a salute in bourbon."

Utah said eagerly, "I was never so thirsty in my life."

They had dinner and rode out. They were mounted on fine big Kentucky horses that rode like rocking chairs. Utah said, "If you ever get the *moro* broke, he may make a horse as good as one of these."

On the second morning out, they made sure that their carbines and pistols were fully loaded. They followed some streams and cut across others. Stuart ticked them off in his mind by name as they approached them and as they left them.

They camped early, using a fire of buffalo chips to avoid smoke. They cooked their supper and made coffee, then covered over the fire and moved on a few miles to camp.

On the third day, they were filing down a deep *arroyada* approaching the Whitefish, with Utah in the lead, when Utah's Army horse suddenly snorted and reared.

Utah swore. "Confounded plug! Damned Army horses always—"

An arrow flashed between Utah and the horse's head. Stuart stopped his own mount abruptly and lay low on the horse's neck. He saw a feather rising in the blackjack above the *arroyada* and fired his six-shooter, aiming six inches below the feather. It disappeared.

Utah could not get his horse stopped, and finally spurred it on down the gulch, for the bed of the creek was in sight. Stuart followed at a hard gallop and hoped there would be no loose stones.

Half a dozen arrows passed over and around them, but they got into the open. It wasn't a very safe spot because the creek bed was not over a hundred yards wide, but it was better than the *arroyada*, which was only about fifteen feet wide.

They turned their horses at a gallop and headed downstream. Then Utah pulled up with an explosive "Damn!" and reversed his horse and started back upstream.

Stuart saw a small village—perhaps seven or eight tepees—of Indians in a narrow section of the stream bed. He saw several squaws and some children—the children standing, the squaws running. And, as he looked, one tepee came tumbling down.

He wheeled and followed Utah. Squaws could shoot as straight as warriors—and sometimes did. And no matter how much he would like to get rid of a few more redskins, he wasn't going to charge an entire village.

They pounded back up the stream bed. No doubt the Indians at the *arroyada* were sentries; otherwise there would have been more of an attack against them.

He looked up and saw three Indians running out of the *arroyada* on foot, heading toward them. Then they faded into the brush. Utah drew up his horse. "Run the gauntlet?" he shouted.

Stuart was undecided. He didn't like to give them a broadside shot.

Utah swung back. "We might get through. They was just lookouts to protect the village."

"Let's cross the creek," said Stuart.

They splashed across the shallow creek at a gallop, the horses' hoofs throwing water thirty feet.

"Turn upstream," Utah said. "There's more in the brush!"

They galloped for a mile, until the little valley narrowed. Stuart pulled up to give the horses a rest.

"The second bunch didn't shoot at us," he said breathlessly.

"No, they was just stationed to protect the village. There's no warriors in the village."

"I suppose they're out stealing cattle and killing whites," Stuart observed.

Utah glanced at him curiously. "Maybe."

"I'll report the village to Miles. The soldiers will clean it out in a hurry."

"They'll be gone by the time the soldiers get there," Utah said. "You can be sure those tepees are already down."

"Won't they fight?"

"What with?" asked Utah. "There was nothing there but squaws and young'uns."

"I've seen squaws kill."

"Only when they had to. Squaws aren't any better fighters than white women."

They found a trail out of the valley and went up on the west side of the creek. A cavalry patrol was trotting across the buffalo grass with a second lieutenant in charge.

Stuart and Utah pulled up and waited. The young lieutenant had been in the West long enough to glance at the brands on their horses. "Come from Fort Sill?" he asked.

"That's right," said Stuart, waiting but full of curiosity.

"Going where?"

"To see Miles."

The lieutenant nodded. "I'm Lieutenant Jones, Sixth Cavalry."

"Stuart Nichols, Rocking Seven, and Utah Thompson."

"Pleased to meet a white man out here. You fellows seen any Indians?"

"Downstream about two miles," said Stuart.

"How many tepees?"

"Seven or eight," said Utah, "but they'll be gone by now."

The young lieutenant grinned. "Squaws and kids with 'em?"

"Yes," said Stuart.

"We'll find 'em," the lieutenant said positively. "They'll leave a trail we can follow. Eight lodges would be about forty Indians."

"Cheyennes," said Utah.

"That means fifteen to twenty fighting men. Well, they're practically out of powder and lead. I don't think we'll have any trouble. We'll wipe out the whole bunch." He looked around at his patrol. "You men wanta see some squaws beg?"

Some of the men nodded.

"They scatter like rats in a woodpile when we hit them," the lieutenant said. "But it takes them too long to gather up the kids. We generally get most of them."

Stuart asked slowly, "You kill squaws and babies too?"

"Sure. The squaws make more Indians; the babies grow up. We kill 'em all. That's the only way to settle it." He looked back at his six men. "I think we're going to have some fun in about an hour. This is better sport than buffalo." He looked at Stuart. "You fellows want to go along?"

Stuart said, "No, we've got to find Miles."

The lieutenant pointed. "About two miles over the hills, there, you'll find the colonel. Sure you won't go along? We'll have them wiped out in two hours."

"We can't delay," said Stuart.

"All right." The lieutenant raised his fist above his head and pumped it a couple of times. *"For-waard! Yo!"*

Stuart kicked his horse ahead. After a while he asked, "How many warriors do you suppose there were to defend that village?"

Utah figured it out. "Four above and four below—not over eight."

"Well, I suppose it's fair enough—eight against seven."

Utah nodded without looking at him. "A bow and arrow doesn't shine against a rifle."

They rode into Miles's camp—row after row of tents and picket lines.

Miles was a big man with a huge mustache. "You're a freighter, I understand."

"Part-time freighter. My father owns the Rocking Seven southwest of here in the Tesecato Canyon, and I work out of there."

"This little war must be getting close to your place."

"It's not over forty or fifty miles from here by a beeline—though we haven't seen any Indians in the Tesecato so far."

"Don't be astonished if you do," Miles warned.

"Major Whitehead told me to tell you about the lead up on the Llano."

Miles listened. Then he sat back in his camp chair, thoughtful. "We need that lead ourselves." He looked at a map. "It would be particularly unfortunate if the Indians, having captured six hundred pounds of gunpowder, could now lay hands on the lead. One of our big advantages at the moment is the fact that they are extremely short of ammunition and dare not risk a large-scale engagement."

"The Indians never have fought large-scale engagements," said Stuart. "Do you think they would now if they had the ammunition?"

"Stone Calf of the Cheyennes is a very smart chief, and some of our small engagements recently give us cause to think he not only has persuaded his warriors to fight white-man style but that he has actually been training them."

Stuart was silent, thinking.

"If that kind of thing happens, our soldiers are no match for the Indians. Two-thirds of our men are youngsters from the East, inexperienced at any kind of frontier fighting. We're outnumbered and we would be outfought. It is conceivable that one major victory for Stone Calf would spread like wild-fire through the Territory. If it did, every Indian on the reservations would rush to the Panhandle, and there would be the greatest massacre the world has ever seen—with our scalps as the prizes."

Stuart frowned. "Is it actually true you could lose this war in the Panhandle?"

"Our entire presence here is based on the premise that Indians will continue to fight as Indians have always fought. If they turned, they could win—and it would require, con-servatively, twenty years for us to win it back."

"And, if that happened, our ranches wouldn't be worth much."

"Not to you," said Miles. "I would think the breaks east of the Caprock would be a regular fortress for the Indians under such a circumstance. That is their historic home, you know. Every canyon along there with any water in it was once an Indian refuge."

Stuart took a deep breath. "We'd better get that lead, then."

Miles looked at his map on the wall of the tent. "You think you know where the lead is?"

Stuart went over to the map as Miles got up. He studied it for a moment, then pointed to a spot some fifty miles south-west of the *puerta* at the Rocking Seven. "No farther than that, I would guess. We were half a day from a small lake, which could have been this one."

Miles looked at Utah. "Weren't you scouting for Carson in 'sixty-eight?"

"I was attached to Fort Dodge," said Utah. "Scouted for different ones."

"You know what this Indian fighting is like, then?"

Utah shook his head. "No more'n this feller does."

"Between you," said Miles, "you ought to be able to find the lead—"

"I'm sure we can," said Stuart.

"—before the Indians find it."

"Once *we* get up there," said Stuart, "it won't be easy for them to hunt it."

"That's a good hard day's ride from your place."

"About."

"If we assume this man Fisher went directly to Stone Calf and told him about the lead—and it would not be the first time a white man has tried to cash in on an Indian victory—then the Indians must already be looking for the lead."

"It won't be easy to find," Stuart said, "unless they have a lot of men with plenty of time and perfect freedom. In the first place, they will waste a day or two scouring the Llano for Fisher's grubbing hoe. Only after they are sure that is gone will they change their method of search."

Miles sat down again. "Then there would be the problem of getting it out of the ground. The only thing I can think of Stone Calf doing is digging a big hole alongside it and building a fire to melt it down a little at a time. Then he could break off the rivulets, so to speak."

"That takes time," said Stuart, "a lot of time."

"If you will wait until my patrols come in tonight, I will send a couple of platoons with you." Miles went out and talked to one of his captains, then came back. "Perhaps day after tomorrow. Can you wait over?"

Stuart said, "Since our place is right on the way, we'd as soon go on home, Colonel, this afternoon. Your men won't have any trouble finding us—and it will give me a day or so at the ranch. The work is already way behind, and November is crowding us."

"All right. I will send a detail out tomorrow or the next day at the latest. They will have orders to stay with you until you find the lead, and then to help you recover it. Satisfactory?"

"Fine." Stuart got up. "Thank you, Colonel. We'll ride on."

"Sure you won't stay for dinner?"

"Yes."

"Very well. You—"

"Colonel!" The captain stuck his head through the tent door. "Sir, I know you'll be delighted with this news. Lieutenant Jones has just returned from a patrol down the creek. He surprised a village of Cheyennes, and they packed up their lodges and tried to escape, but he followed. He killed every one of them! Twenty-eight Indians!"

Miles' eyes narrowed. "How many warriors?"

"Six, sir."

"Twenty-two squaws and children, then." Miles bit his lip and looked at the floor. Then he recovered himself and looked up at Stuart and Utah. "War is a bloody business, gentlemen."

Stuart frowned. "Is it the Army's policy to kill women and children?"

Miles said, "No, it is not—but in the heat of battle it is often difficult to tell a warrior from a squaw. They both dress in buckskin, you know."

CHAPTER X

THEY were silent on the way home. They·camped in a draw that night without a fire. Miles did not think they would be attacked in the open, but he had loaned them two fresh horses to ride. They still trailed their own, and if they were attacked they could change horses and most likely outrun the Indians, for Miles had reported that the Cheyenne horses were in poor condition following the long, dry summer with the Indians constantly on the move. Mackenzie had captured and killed some 2,000 Comanche horses in the Palo Duro less than a month before, and it was believed the Comanches who escaped had gone to other bands and thus put an additional drain on the horse herds.

They descended the eastern Caprock of the Tesecato shortly after noon, down an ancient Indian trail. George was waiting for them long before they crossed the flat and got into the creek bottom.

"How are things going?" asked Stuart, shaking hands.

"Fine. You fellers run into any trouble?"

"Nothing serious. Heard from Fisher?"

"One of his hands was up lookin' for a couple of steers, but I don't think he missed anything. I figgered he was scoutin' the lay of the land."

Stuart dismounted. "You didn't say anything?"

"We just let him talk."

Stuart nodded. "The military doesn't want to arrest him yet. It's up to us to give him enough rope to hang himself, but if we catch him dead to rights I guess we better take care of him ourselves."

71

They unsaddled their horses and turned them out to graze. George asked, "You see the shoulder straps?"

"We saw them."

"What's the verdict?"

"It's serious," said Stuart, throwing his saddle on a fence. "Serious all the way around. Colonel Miles thinks if the Indians win, we won't have any ranch up here any longer."

George, braced on his crutches, said stubbornly, "I ain't moving. I been moving all my life, and this is one time I stay put."

"You won't have much choice if the Cheyennes take over."

"I'll stay right here until they lift my scalp," George said. "I'm too old to be startin' over somewhere else."

"We would get some indemnity from the government," Stuart suggested.

"Maybe. Also when the gover'ment gets good and ready. I seen men wait years for that kind of money."

Stuart slapped him on the shoulder. "There's plenty in the same boat, Dad. Meantime, let's all do the best we can."

They went inside. The cook said, "I was half expectin' you. It happened there was a little biscuit dough left over. Would you like some hot ones?"

Stuart sighed. "Sounds good."

"Miz Schooler was up and left a jar of peach preserves her mother sent her. You think you'd like to try 'em?"

Stuart said, "It sounds almost as good as biscuits." Then he turned to his father. "How's Brisket?"

"Ain't heard no complaint."

"He kinda lost track of things up on the Llano."

George shuddered. "It ain't human. You can't blame any man for goin' to pieces in that wind."

"Nobody did."

Utah began to hunt for his plug. Stuart leaned back to roll a cigarette. "You said Miz Schooler brought the peach preserves," he said, keeping his eye on the cigarette. "Everything all right down there?"

"No report otherwise," said George, probing with his sharp blue eyes.

Stuart and Utah filled up on biscuits and preserves, and George had a couple to top off his dinner. "We'll go ahead with our work until sometime tomorrow, probably," said Stuart. "There'll be a patrol from the Army here then, and we'll go back up on the Llano. I'll want Brisket and Dusty and

Pablo, same as before, for I got a hunch that lead isn't going to be easy to locate unless we're lucky."

"You marked it, didn't you?"

"Sure I did—but you know what the Llano is like. One acre looks exactly like five million other acres up there. And of course we were lost when we cached the stuff."

"How long will you be gone?" asked George.

"Three or four days or a week."

"We'll make out down here. There's nothin' important."

"Then I think this afternoon I'll work on the *moro* stallion," said Stuart.

Nine of the mules had drifted back home. Two were down at Buckley's Toadfrog, and a couple were up in Clarendon County. Probably some of them were up on the Llano— coyote bait.

Stuart went outside and stretched. The sun was shining down into the Tesecato on the warm October day. The lemon yellow leaves of the cottonwoods were dropping; the time of northers was not far off, but the air was quiet and balmy, mellow—not hot, not cool. The breeze flowed from the Llano down through the Tesecato Canyon.

George came out on his crutches. "I'll get back to my harness work for a while," he said.

Stuart nodded. He went over to the pen where Slim had brought up the *moro*. The mulberry-colored stallion stood in the center of the pen, head and tail high.

Stuart lifted a coiled rope from a fence post and climbed over the gate. He shook out the rope and tossed a loop over the *moro's* head, and eased the snubbing-rope steadily so the horse could run in a circle.

After a while he let the horse cool off while he squatted on the ground near the gate, the rope loose.

The Caprock stood high and immovable on the west. To the southeast, the Tesecato widened out into the breaks about where Fisher's spread started. The breaks was a rough area of gypsum water and hard travel, of sterile, rocky soil, baked century after century under a blazing sun. But up in the canyon there was always a breeze funneled down from the Llano; the grass grew thick and green, and deer browsed among the cedar trees at the base of the Caprock or at the foot of the bluff on the opposite side.

Stuart sat there looking up toward the Caprock, with its red and rust, brown and blue colors. The top was as flat as a poker table, but the weaving edge gave the impression of turrets and towers, ancient and inscrutable.

He wondered, squatting there, how many generations of Indians of how many tribes had camped down there in the Tesecato, long before the Spaniards came, and had looked up there at that same Caprock. What had they seen? he wondered. Not towers, of course, because they had not known about towers.

Thinking about it and gazing idly down the canyon, he noted the movement of a big white horse two or three miles down, and observed that Pablo was driving half a dozen buffalo on down the canyon to save the grass. Then he looked back at the *moro,* saw it was getting wound up on the snubbing-post and loosened up the rope.

He got up reluctantly, and it struck him that after three weeks in the saddle he was tired.

The rope ran too fast through his hands, and, while he followed the *moro* around the post, he reached with his right hand for the horsehide gloves in his hip pocket. Then he heard hoofbeats and looked up. He glanced at his gun-belt hanging on a post at the gate, then put his bare hand back on the rope.

John Fisher rode up by the gate, and Stuart took a deep breath. Fisher said, "I heard you been to Fort Sill."

"Yes."

"Any news about the Indians?"

From where Stuart stood he could see George and Utah watching from the harness shed, the cook from the kitchen. "Nothing important," he said. "The campaign goes on."

Fisher paused. "I thought maybe you wanted to know how I felt about what happened out there."

"I wasn't worried," Stuart said, "except that we're neighbors, and as long as we have ranches as close as we have, it's easier to be on speaking terms than not."

"I don't hold it against you—the things you said."

Stuart stared at him for an instant. The man was a strange mixture of twisted impulses to do right and of downright orneriness, and sometimes it was hard to separate the two. At this moment, perhaps, he had come to try to make amends in a clumsy way for what had happened, and also to get back on Stuart's good side, for undoubtedly he was painfully aware that Stuart could damage him by telling what had happened on the Llano. The strangest thing of all was that

74

Fisher didn't think he had already reported—but then a man like Fisher figured things out in his own twisted way.

Fisher was riding a long-legged bay. "That Mex ridin' the bog down there by the lower springs—"

So it had changed already. Fisher now figured that he had put things back on a level basis, and he would pick up from there.

Stuart looked up from under his big hat. He said, "You know by this time his name is Pablo."

"Whatever his name is."

Stuart looked at him as he kept the rope tight on the *moro*. Then he turned back to the stallion, noting that its natural restlessness had increased when Fisher approached; now it was loping around the snubbing-post, and Stuart had to watch to keep up with him. "Pablo works for me," Nichols said. "He worked for my father down in Sonora."

"He's a greaser, ain't he?" Fisher demanded.

Yes, it was like a man of Fisher's stripe. Now that he had, in his own mind, settled all other things between them, he went ahead with his attack.

Watching the *moro* with one eye and keeping pace with the horse around the post, Stuart looked up.

Fisher needed a shave, as usual. His hat was drooping at the left, and he looked like a steer with broken horns just come in out of a rainstorm. A blue bandanna was tied under his reddish whiskers. The only thing about him that looked good to Nichols was the bay. They hardly ever saw a horse of that size around the Caprock, for most of the big horses were eastern horses and didn't take to alkali water and prairie grass. Nichols said finally, "Pablo's a white man and he works for me."

Fisher snorted. "No Mexican is a white man no matter who he works for."

Stuart said, "You never liked Pablo."

"I never trusted him."

Stuart followed the rope around the post. "I never trusted *you*," he said.

"Damn you," said Fisher, "I'll clean your plow yet for talkin' to me like that."

"If you do," said Stuart, "it'll be the first fair fight you ever were in."

Fisher snorted again. "I come down here to make peace talk—and you want to fight."

75

Stuart shrugged. "Not necessarily. I'm not running from it, though." He glanced at Fisher. "Don't move toward my gun-belt. You're covered from the kitchen and from the harness shed."

Fisher sat back in his saddle, red with anger. "Let's use some sense."

"You can begin by not calling Pablo a greaser."

Stuart lengthened his rope until he got out to the wall of the pen; there he slipped a pole that served as a gate. He dropped it to the ground, and the *moro* came to the opening and tried to turn into it. Stuart went up the rope to its head and unfastened the rope from the halter. The *moro* made a half-hearted nip at him and then charged through into the other pen.

"I could teach you something about breaking horses," Fisher said. "If I had that *moro,* I'd climb on him with a whip, and when I got through he wouldn't never feel like pitchin' again."

Stuart watched the mulberry stallion crowhop across the corral a couple of times and circle back, head tossing. He walked to the gate, ignoring Fisher's remark about breaking the horse. He dropped his gun-belt around his hips and fastened the buckle. "You ever touch that horse with a whip, Fisher, you're in plenty of trouble."

Fisher looked sullen. "I know you been blaming me for everything that happened on the Llano."

"You practically admitted it by taking my horse and leaving."

"What else could I do? Your men might have hung me if they had taken a notion."

Stuart asked, with curiosity, "You have any other idea about who's giving information to the Indians?"

"I know one thing," Fisher said doggedly. "They could raid down here if somebody gave 'em a signal."

Stuart looked up. "What kind of signal?"

"A few green cottonwood leaves on a branding fire could be seen for fifteen mile up on the Llano."

"Are you connecting Pablo with that?" Stuart demanded.

"Why's he always workin' around the bog?"

Stuart crawled between the poles of the gate. "Because he's the best bog hand in the Panhandle."

"And maybe because he can see down to my place and

up here at the same time. When the coast is clear in both places he can give a signal."

"Why would he want to do that?"

"Them Mexicans will do anything to get the best of an *anglo*."

Stuart faced him angrily. "Mexicans are just like *anglos*— some good and some bad. Some mighty bad."

Fisher began to turn red under his whiskers. "What do you mean by that?" he demanded. "I come down here to make peace."

"If it sounded nasty," Stuart said, "it sounded the way I meant it. We live in the same canyon and I'm willing to be on speaking terms with you, but I still don't like your looks."

Fisher left his saddle in a flying leap. Stuart moved to one side and turned his shoulder forward in time to catch Fisher in the stomach. Fisher hit the ground and jumped up, swinging.

Stuart stepped back, and Fisher crowded him against the fence. Stuart ducked in under his big arms and hit Fisher in the stomach twice and slipped off to one side.

Fisher, breathing hard, came after him. Over Fisher's shoulder, Stuart saw the cook standing in the door with a rifle. He wheeled and started to belt Fisher in the face, but a haymaker came from somewhere and slammed him down. He caught two more on the way, and then his face was in dust that smelled of horse. He raised his head and saw Fisher waiting. He took another deep breath and leaped to his feet, head down.

Fisher stepped back, so most of the force of Stuart's drive was gone when he hit him. Fisher slugged him twice more in the face before Stuart got his head up, and then Stuart was straightened with one on the chin, and sat down.

He took his time getting up, and when he did get up he watched himself. When Fisher swung, he wasn't there. But he waded back in at the right second and began to chop the big man down. Stuart was outweighed by forty pounds, but he was as hard as three years with Mosby, sixteen months under Maximilian and five years in the Texas Rangers could make him, and he'd had a week to recover from the Llano. When his fist connected, it sounded like a fulminate cap.

Fisher, rocked by blows that he never saw, began to bleed from cuts on the face, and he stumbled as he moved back and forth and tried to pin Stuart down.

77

"Stand up an' fight!" he growled.

Stuart didn't answer, but continued to hammer the man with his fists. Fisher wavered. Stuart hit him twice, and Fisher went down.

Stuart watched him for a moment as Fisher rose to a sitting position and wiped the blood from his mouth.

"You said all you had on your mind?" asked Stuart.

Fisher glared at him. Slowly he got to his feet, climbed into his saddle and galloped out of the yard.

Stuart watched him disappear around the first clump of mesquite, and took a deep breath. He glanced back at the *moro,* standing with its intelligent-looking head over the gate between the two pens, its ears twitching, nostrils quivering. Stuart relaxed a little. The *moro* would make a great horse some day.

Stuart turned toward the harness-shed. He ducked his head under the cottonwood log that served as the top of the door-frame that led into the walled end and went inside, stamping his boots on the hard-packed dirt floor. He turned to the left, swished the big tin dipper in the pail, brought it up dripping and drank deeply.

"I thought for a minute there you and Fisher were about to settle things for good," said George.

Stuart grunted. He lowered the dipper and took a breath. "For a minute I thought so myself," he said. Then he finished the water, tossed a few drops through the open door and hung the dipper on a nail. He looked across the open doorway at the white-haired man sitting before a saddle on the wooden horse. Two waxed threads hung from the saddle-skirt, and the older man was punching holes with an awl.

Then he glanced at the Smith & Wesson lever-action across the older man's lap. "You better not go getting mixed up in this," he said. "You're a sitting duck if anybody comes after you."

The elder Nichols slid the rifle off his legs and stood it against the door-frame. "Not while I can shoot," he said.

Stuart frowned.

"I don't figure that feller," said George. "He come in just like nothin' ever happened up there on the Llano."

"It's his style," said Stuart.

"He's as dangerous as a rattlesnake," said George.

"More so," said Stuart. "You *know* a rattlesnake is going to strike you if you get too close. You don't know *anything*

78

if you pay attention to Fisher, because he doesn't know himself."

His father said, "Stuart, there's others think he's right about the *moro*."

Stuart looked up. "Somebody wants to rough-break the stallion?"

The older man looked at him steadily. "I heard somebody wonder if you're afraid to fork him."

Stuart pushed his hat back on his head. "It beats me how everybody always knows more about a man's business than he knows himself."

His father took up a waxed thread. "Way it goes," he noted.

"Why didn't somebody else tie into that horse up at Wichita when he was waiting to be shipped to the glue factory? Everybody passed him up until I came along and offered five dollars for him."

The elder Nichols put the thread through the hole and twisted it again between his thumb and forefinger. "They never took the trouble to look in his mouth. He was so bony they figgered he was thirty years old."

"They were mighty poor men around a corral," said Stuart. "Look what three months of corn did for him." He stopped to watch the *moro* for a minute. "See that coat? As glossy as a Kentucky walking horse."

George spoke defensively. "I just told you what they said."

Stuart said, "Anybody who touches that horse is in trouble. You can tell them that for me. I'll Indian-break him if I like—and when I get through I'll have a horse they'd give their eyeteeth for."

There was a hard smack from above, and loose dirt dropped from the top of the door-frame. Stuart stared for an instant. Then he dodged back from the open doorway. His father was holding the Smith & Wesson against the door-frame. Utah Thompson, who never seemed to move fast, somehow had materialized from the depths of the shed and was standing back a little from the doorway so he wouldn't be in the sunlight, with his Henry carbine in his hands.

Then the distant report of a rifle shot reached them.

Stuart, standing back in the shadow, looked out over the lower canyon. "I don't see Fisher. It might have been an accident."

Utah drawled, "Any bullet that comes that close is no accident."

79

George said, "You can gener'ly make out Fisher for two miles through that mesquite—but I haven't seen him for some time. He must have gotten off to walk. He laid his rifle across the saddle and took a pot-shot at us."

"What for?"

"Hard to say—feller like Fisher. It might be he just wanted to chouse us up a little."

Utah set down his rifle and went through a small doorway at the end of the shed. In a moment Stuart heard his slow, measured blows as he carved out a cottonwood axle-tree with an adze.

"Why doesn't he come out in the open? What's he beating around the bush for? If he wants to be bad, why doesn't he pull a six-shooter?"

The elder Nichols, on his crutches, helped himself to a drink of water. "You been too long in a world where everything's cut and dried."

"I don't know what you mean."

"In the Rangers you was dealing with outlaws. A man was either on the side of the law or against it. No halfway."

"Sure."

"You got something else to deal with now—a man with a respectable front but a crooked inside."

"In the meantime it isn't going to be easy living in the same valley with a man like Fisher."

The elderly man pointed with a crutch. A head was bobbing in the tall bushes about a mile away. "I'll tell you this—any law-abidin' man dealing with Fisher has got to absorb a lot, because Fisher will take at least the limit of the law every time."

Stuart hung the snubbing rope on a peg.

George stood for a moment, balanced on his crutches. "I think I'll sashay up to the ranch house and take a snooze," he said.

He set out for the two-story adobe two hundred yards away. The harness-shed, the main ranch house and the corrals formed a triangle on the flat above the mesquite thicket.

Stuart walked with him. The way the elderly man swung his useless leg made Stuart wonder if he'd be able to navigate across the yard—but he always did. They reached the kitchen door, and Stuart turned away, saying, "The soldiers will be here tomorrow and I'll have to go back up on the Llano; I think I'd better saddle up the gray and look things over this afternoon."

He had reached the middle of the open space when he heard a shout from the kitchen and then a hoarse cry from the harness-shed. He wheeled. Then his father shouted:

"Christopher! Where'd them Injuns come from?"

Stuart turned back sharply, hearing the ululating cry of the Cheyennes. He looked up at the east wall of the canyon and saw them streaming out from the base of the wall. He stared for an instant. The Indians were riding single file on horses of many colors. They wore single feathers in their hair; their brown bodies were naked from the waist up, covered with buckskin leggings from the waist down. They broke into the flat northeast of the ranch yard and began to spread out on a broad front.

Utah Thompson shouted from the harness shed. "Take cover, you idiot!"

Stuart raised his pistol and fired three times in the air. He started to run for the house, but, remembering Utah was alone in the harness-shed, he turned that way.

CHAPTER XI

UTAH was waiting inside with his carbine.

Stuart took a box of cartridges from a shelf and filled the six-shooter hurriedly. "Must be twenty-five or thirty of 'em."

"If we hold 'em off for half an hour," Utah said, "the boys will come in from the south and give us a hand."

Stuart said grimly, "These Indians must be after scalps."

"It don't make sense," said Utah. "They're fightin' the U.S. Army and they take time out for a raid down here. Nope, I don't think they come for scalps."

"What for, then?"

Utah shook his head. He was steadying his rifle, following the first Indian on the near side.

"Maybe they're looking for supplies," said Stuart.

The long file of Indians, coming on at a hard gallop, was just breaking out of the brush onto the flat four hundred yards away.

"We might stand 'em off, at that," Utah noted. "Your dad and the cook and Brisket up at the house. You and me here."

Stuart chucked the six-shooter in his holster and picked up his father's Smith & Wesson. "Recognize any of them?" he asked.

"That ugly one there—second from the front—looks like Six Arrows, one of Stone Calf's outfit. But what are they raidin' for? They know Mackenzie and the cavalry is lookin' for 'em all over the Panhandle. Miles is only a day's ride away. You wouldn't think they would invite trouble."

"They would if there is something they need," said Stuart. "And if they thought they could find it here."

Less than two hundred yards away now, the Indians formed two columns and swept down toward the ranch house. Their hollow yells rolled across the hard-baked clay and sent a shiver down Stuart's backbone.

"There'll be hair raised today," Utah muttered, drawing a bead.

A dull thud came from the house. A half-naked Indian lurched to the off-side of his horse. He hung there a moment and then catapulted headfirst onto the ground.

Stuart said, "Dad got his old army pistol working!"

A sharper crack sounded beside him. Utah growled, "Missed him—but got the horse."

The horse had gone down on one leg. The Cheyenne rolled off. He got to his feet running, saw the riderless horse behind, threw himself against its neck and a moment later was riding.

The two columns separated to go around the house. A shower of arrows suddenly blossomed in the closed kitchen door. Rifle shots sounded from the windows of the house.

Stuart turned his head a little sidewise. "You hear those shots?"

"You think I'm a gate post?" asked Utah.

"They were sharp cracks. It doesn't sound like these Indians are short of gunpowder."

Utah nodded. "Good guess. Then they're after lead or food —and they aren't fooling. They got instructions to shoot the limit."

Stuart was puzzled. "Why not wait till night and try to steal? An attack in broad daylight—they ought to know it won't work."

"Indians think funny sometimes."

"Not that funny."

The two columns swung together, then apart, and cut a tight circle. One column galloped around the front of the ranch house while the other marked time.

Stuart pulled the trigger of the Smith & Wesson. The Cheyenne who had remounted looked suddenly surprised. A big red spot appeared in his left side, about halfway between his shoulder and his elbow. Then he crumpled. He slid over the horse's rump and hit the ground flat on his back.

The two columns met again in front of the house and hesitated, milling, while the leaders conferred. A brown-faced warrior wearing two feathers swooped down at a gallop and leaned over to snatch up the wounded Indian. Utah's rifle cracked, and the riding Indian slid off the horse and piled on top of the one on the ground.

Stuart, watching the confab, said, "They've spotted us out here. Half of them will come this way in a minute."

Utah took a drink of water. "There ought to be some help comin' up pretty soon from the pasture," he said hopefully.

Stuart drank the rest of the dipperful and dropped the dipper in the bucket.

Utah said grimly, "If they'd cut out them fancy cavalry shenanigans and rush us, you and me'd last about one half a minute, Texas time."

Stuart looked down the canyon. "Even Fisher's men won't stand by and see us massacred," he said, without really believing it.

Utah slid two cartridges into his rifle. "I'm glad we got other friends."

The Cheyennes started in a circle. Two pointers led out, each followed by a column. One file started around the house. The other file, whooping their war cry, charged toward the harness-shed.

"Don't shoot too soon," Stuart said.

Shots came from the house, but the column swinging around from the other side answered them with arrows and rifles. Then the second column, having swung to the left to keep out of range of the harness-shed door, swerved at the end of the shed and galloped toward the door, single file.

Utah fired. Stuart centered his pistol on the chest of Six Arrows and pulled the trigger. A red spot appeared on the Indian's chest, but the Cheyenne drew his war bow and an arrow flashed between Utah and Stuart and buried itself in the far wall with an ugly thud.

Stuart shot the Indian again, going away. That was one Cheyenne, he thought grimly, that wouldn't raid again anywhere. The Indian half-circled his horse and released another arrow, which buried its hoop-iron head in the door-frame with an ominous *thunk* and quivered for a moment just above Stuart's pistol. Stuart fired again. The Cheyenne finally lost his hold on his horse and went into the dirt on all fours.

Two other Indians were on the ground. Utah, hiding as far as possible behind the wall of the shed, was firing left-handed to keep from exposing himself. There were arrows in the

84

door-frame, half a dozen in the far wall and several scattered on the floor.

Utah said through the white smoke, "You see the hoop-iron heads? Those are war arrows, all right."

Stuart said shortly, "I thought maybe they were playing games."

Utah said, without looking around, "It means they planned this. It didn't just happen."

"With Six Arrows leading, I figured as much."

The Indians swept out of sight for a moment. Utah got in a last shot that slapped a horse in the rump.

Stuart reloaded.

Utah said, "Gimme a pocketful of cartridges."

Stuart dropped a dozen shells into Utah's extended hand. Utah was watching the Indians. "They got three from the house," Stuart said with satisfaction.

Utah looked at him through the lifting powder smoke. "Now there's only twenty-two," he said.

They swept past the shed again. One more Indian fell. Arrows slid through the dust and the smoke, through the open doorway, into the frame. The Indians wheeled again. The air in the shed was almost too acrid for breathing.

Suddenly cries came from down the canyon.

"Pablo and Andy!" said Utah. "I always did say that them two was the whitest men in the Panhandle."

The Indians milled for a moment. Pablo was fogging his big white horse at a hard gallop. Behind him came Andy, the Negro hand, beating his old sorrel gelding over the rump with his hat.

The Indians, confused at this sudden all-out frontal attack by two men from an unexpected quarter, and probably wondering how many more were coming behind them, started yelling at one another. In a moment they had wheeled in three different circles and galloped behind the breaking corral, and were pulling their horses to a ploughing stop.

They were out of pistol range, but Stuart threw a shot for luck and began to give them back their own war cry.

The Cheyennes held their horses back. Then a lone rider wheeled out from behind the posts. His horse, a bay-and-white paint, pawed the air for a moment. The Cheyenne kicked it into a hard gallop and suddenly dropped behind the horse, his heel in a sling at the crude saddlehorn, to snatch up a wounded warrior.

Utah said, "I hate to do this," but pulled the trigger.

The horse stopped, ploughing up earth. Its haunches went down. It tried to get up, but its front legs collapsed. The Indian slid off. He threw the wounded man over his shoulder and started to run back. Two shots sounded from the house, and the Indian spread out on the ground and lay still, the other Indian still on his back.

"That's Six Arrows," said Utah. "He's so full of lead they ought to take him back to Stone Calf and melt him down."

Pablo and Andy were less than a quarter of a mile away now, and half a mile behind them appeared two more, their whoops faint but carrying on the still air.

"Sounds like Dusty and Slim," said Utah, watching the Cheyennes.

The Cheyennes hesitated. Then, with a shout, they wheeled their horses and cut around behind the wagon-shed, out of range, to make a run for the trail down which they had come.

Utah wiped the sweat from his face with his red bandanna. "Close work," he said, "for a hot day like this."

Stuart walked out of the door, his six-shooter in his hand.

"Keep an eye on them dead Injuns," said Utah.

Stuart said, "I'm not worried about Six Arrows. I wonder if anybody got hurt up at the house."

He set out across the hard-baked ground, now broken up by the pounding hoofs of the Cheyenne horses. He noted that some of them had been shod, so they must have been recently stolen. That didn't mean much, of course, for horses changed hands fast in the Panhandle when Indians were on the prod.

"Duck!" shouted Utah.

Stuart ducked and swung around. Smoke was coming from the breaking corral. Six Arrows was up on his knees. He had just set a match to the dry tumbleweeds caught against the bottom of the fence, perhaps in the hope of getting at the *moro,* but now, discovered, he straightened up on his knees. Blood poured from his mouth, and his chest was covered with red foam, but he drew his bow and let an arrow fly. It whirred by in front of Stuart at eye level, missing him by about a foot. The Indian already had another arrow to his bow, and, as he let it go, Stuart carefully shot him between the eyes.

Utah ran out of the shed. "Got more life than a buffalo bull." He ran up to the Indian with a knife. He bent over, and, when he straightened up, he had a bloody scalp in one hand.

86

He wiped the blade of his bowie knife on his old leather pants. "They come for a scalpin'," he said defensively.

"It's good enough for them." Stuart kicked dirt on the fire. He didn't mind cremating the Indian, but he had enough to do without rebuilding the corral.

His father had the door open at the ranch house. "You two all right?" he asked.

"We're here," said Utah.

George, leaning heavily on his crutches, got back to his chair. "Cookee and me are whole," he said, "but Brisket got a Minié ball in his right eye."

The white-aproned, long-mustached cook looked down at them from where he stood on a hogshead of flour, a single-shot Maynard in his hands. "It went clean through," he said, "and took most of his brains with it."

Pounding hoofs came into the yard. Pablo slid off the white horse and ran into the kitchen, his brown face taut, his black eyes alive, glancing from one to the other. *"Son todos buenos?"* he asked.

Andy, right behind him, was looking at the floor. "I reckon all but Mistah Brisket. He don't look so good over there."

Pablo stared at the mutilated body, his eyes wide. He crossed himself hurriedly.

The cook blew smoke from his rifle and got down from the flour barrel. "I better clean up the muss," he said, "so we can bury him."

Utah, in the door, was watching the Cheyennes climb the canyon wall. "It's a doggone funny thing to me," he said, "why they came at this time of day. They gener'ly come early in the morning unless they got information otherwise."

"Did it strike you," asked Stuart, "that that first shot at the harness-shed door was to draw our attention?"

The elder Nichols looked at him absently, his blue eyes narrow. "We were watchin' the pasture while the Cheyennes were comin' from the Caprock."

"They didn't make a move of any kind toward the stock," Stuart noted.

"Except the one that tried to get to the *moro* so he could escape."

Stuart looked around. "Pablo, go put out the fire in the corral fence. Cottonwood doesn't burn easy, but it burns hot. I see it's blazing up out there, so I guess I didn't get it all."

"Sí, señor." Pablo's white teeth flashed and he was gone.

"Now, then," said Stuart, "will somebody give me a hand with this arrow?"

They stared at him. The cook, standing by Brisket's body, looked up questioningly.

Stuart turned around. A foot of bloody arrow shaft stuck out of the back of his thigh. "I cut off the feathers in front," he said, "but I couldn't get ahold of the head."

Utah glanced at the arrow, keen-eyed. He set down his rifle, laid both hands on the shaft and jerked it out with no preliminary.

Stuart grunted, and the cook held out a bottle. "A slug of bourbon will help."

Stuart's mouth was open as he gasped for air, and sweat was running down his face. He took the bottle and tipped it up.

"What I can't figger," said Utah, looking at the bloody arrow, "is when you got this thing."

Stuart lowered the bottle. "You said Six Arrows had more life than a buffalo bull," he reminded Utah. "What did you think he was shootin' at—the chimney?"

Then Stuart sank to the floor, unconscious.

CHAPTER XII

WHEN Stuart opened his eyes again he was lying on a buffalo robe with his pants off. Pablo, on his knees, was bathing his leg with hot water and a piece of worn-out blanket. Utah Thompson was looking out the door, his knife in his hand.

"George, get a can of gunpowder," said the cook.

The elder Nichols, standing on one leg, reached up for the canister. The cook brought a jar of deer-tallow from the back of the stove, and George made a paste of the tallow and the gunpowder. They applied it to the two arrow wounds, one front and one back, made a couple of pads from an old green flannel shirt and tied them in place with a strip of the cloth. Stuart grunted as they tightened the bandage and tied it. He pulled up his pants and buttoned them.

"You'll be all right," his father said. "It went clean through."

"Good thing," drawled Utah. "It was hoop iron. That stuff gives a man blood poisoning." He looked at his knife. "Reckon I'll sashay out there and git me some more souvenirs."

Stuart got up gingerly and tried his weight. His leg hurt, but not too much. He limped to the door and watched Utah make a cut about the size of a dollar around one Indian's scalplock. Utah slipped his knife back in his sheath, put a foot on the Indian's chest, seized the scalplock and jerked. The scalp came loose with a loud pop. Stuart turned back.

George Nichols said, "I got a piece of lead in my arm, cook. Reckon you can fish it out?"

The cook stuffed in his billowed-out shirt tail, looked at Nichols' arm and said, "Sure." He took a hone from the window sill, spat on it, and began to sharpen a paring knife.

Pablo came in smelling of burned wood. He pushed his big hat back. *"Yo tengo vergüenza*—I have shame that I am not here to help," he said.

"We did all right the way it was," said the cook, trying the knife-edge on his thumb.

"A very good fight—no? You get eleven Indians—yes?"

George watched the cook swishing the knife blade in the bottle of Cedar Valley. "I'll take a swig of that when you get through. Andy!"

"Yas, suh."

"You better get the pan. I may bleed like a stuck hog."

Andy got the wash pan, threw the water out the back door, poured a little fresh water in the pan to rinse it and came back.

George looked up at Pablo. "We got plenty of hides," he said, "but we wasted a lot of shells doing it."

Two men ran across the yard from the corrals. "It looks like we got here too late," said Dusty.

George said sourly, "You'd never come so fast if there was post holes to dig."

Slim Lambert, a big, raw-boned boy from Montana who was so tall he went around half folded in the middle to keep his hat from hitting the tops of the door frames, pushed in behind Dusty. "We come up to fight Indians."

George Nichols took a long pull on the bottle of whisky handed him by Andy. He gave it back and said to the cook, "Dig."

Andy slammed the cork back in the bottle and set it up on the shelf. Stuart limped cautiously across the room.

"You'll have to walk on that leg," Dusty said, keen eyes taking in the outline of the bandage under Stuart's pants. "That'll keep it from getting stiff."

Stuart nodded.

Dusty held out the feathered end of an arrow. "I picked this up out in the yard. Is it yourn?"

Stuart nodded.

"Cheyenne, all right," said Dusty.

The cook was digging at George's arm.

"How can you tell?" asked Slim.

"See how the butt end is whittled to a short ridge? See the way the arrows sit close to the shaft? Even the way the red lines run down the shaft."

"They was lookin' for food?" Andy suggested.

"Not the way they went at it."

"No," said Dusty. "They would have snuck down here at night and cut a steer's throat and got out of here." He scratched his head. "No, sir, they was here on business—but what kind of business? Was they lookin' for that lead? With the U. S. Army on their tail all over the Panhandle, you would figger they'd keep out of sight as long as they could."

George Nichols gritted his teeth, and they were all silent for a moment. Then George said, "I noticed the ones that had rifles were shootin' full loads. Generally an Indian is stingy with powder because powder is always scarce, but these boogers' rifles sounded like buffalo hunters. They must be usin' your powder already."

Slim said in his high-mountain twang, "You gents did some fair shootin' to make them leave their dead'uns."

"We had 'em in the middle," the cook said, without turning, "and prob'ly they figgered there was a lot more of us here—the way we was droppin' 'em."

"They'll be back tonight for the corpses," said Slim.

"The bodies won't be here," Stuart told him.

"Anybody watchin' the Caprock to be sure they go all the way?" asked Dusty.

"They went all the way," said Stuart. "They won't be back before sundown."

"Mr. Nichols, what do you figger they was here for?"

There was no answer, and the cook said, without looking around, "He's asleep."

Stuart said fiercely, "Get that slug out of there before he wakes up."

"What do you think I'm doin'? Cuttin' off his arm?"

"You aimin' to dig graves for all them redskins?" asked Slim.

"Hell, no," said Stuart, limping back across the room. His leg hurt like the devil when he stepped on it, but he knew if he babied it he'd be laid up for two weeks.

"You can't leave 'em. They'll draw flies."

Stuart watched the cook for a moment. His father's other arm was twitching. Stuart said, without looking up, "Use a lasso and drag 'em up the trail a ways."

Utah, lean, weather-beaten, and as tough-looking as a chewed piece of rawhide since his two weeks on the Llano, came in with a fistful of bloody scalps. "Ain't had such a good day since I fought the 'Rapahoes up along the Napestle," he said cheerfully.

A horse loped up to the kitchen door and stopped. Dusty stepped outside.

George Nichols groaned. Stuart watched a white line grow around his lips. Then the cook jabbed deep. George twisted, but Andy was holding his shoulder down. The cook brought up his arm slowly and turned to them with a triumphant smile. He held out, on the end of the paring knife, something bloody and as big as the end of a man's thumb.

"About a sixty-caliber Sharps," he said.

Slim drawled, "You got it anyway."

Utah gave George the bottle again. "You need somethin' to live for," he said.

George's eyes closed as he drank. The cook was packing his wound with tallow and powder.

Looking inside, Dusty said, "Anne Schooler's here."

The cook was tying up George's arm with a strip of green cloth as Anne Schooler came in. She was wearing the same man's hat, but this time she had on a red wool shirt that didn't altogether hide the fact that she was a woman. She wore the usual brown wool trousers, boots and spurs. She glanced at Stuart and saw the evidence of the bandages, and the depths of her eyes clouded. "Is it a bad wound?" she asked, seeming almost to flinch as she said the words.

Stuart shook his head. "Clean. Nothin' to it."

She went over to George. "What got you—a bullet?"

George nodded and smiled painfully.

She glanced at the cook and the bloody paring knife. "Did you sterilize that knife?" she demanded.

"Best we could, ma'am. Never lost a man from gangrene yet."

Nobody smiled.

She looked around. "Somebody's missing."

Stuart nodded. "Brisket got it."

She glanced into the front room where Pablo and Slim had laid Brisket's body. She looked back at Stuart and then saw Utah with his handful of scalps. She compressed her lips. "Are you trying to be like them?" she asked.

"No, ma'am," Utah said uncomfortably. Then he pointed out, "I didn't go up there. They came down here."

She drew a deep breath. "Some day," she said, "there will

be civilization down here in the breaks country. How will you account then for the scalps you are taking now?"

Utah looked away through the kitchen window. "Prob'ly," he said, "some Cheyenne'll have my hair tied to a scalp pole."

Anne frowned. Stuart thought she was probably the only woman in the Texas Panhandle who could look beautiful in a frown. She said to Stuart, "What was your wound?"

"Just an arrow," he said, suddenly embarrassed at having attention turned to him.

She touched his arm—so softly he could hardly feel it.

"Does it hurt much?" she asked, watching his eyes.

He smiled down at her. "Not now, ma'am."

She said, "Our men are coming up from the east pasture."

"We won't need 'em," said Stuart. "Andy, go head them back to work. Tell them it's all over."

Andy clumped out.

Utah said, "The rest of our boys are comin' up now."

They heard Dusty shouting news of the attack to half a dozen newcomers. The horses ploughed to a stop near the ranch house, and a cloud of dust rolled on from where they stood.

Stuart walked to the table, favoring his leg considerably, and sat down. "They may come back in the morning."

Utah pulled his hat down harder. "I wouldn't want to be asleep at daybreak."

Anne Schooler whirled on him. "Do you blame them, the way we've taken their land, killed off the buffalo and even killed the Indians?"

Utah looked at her guardedly. "This here is public land, ma'am. It belongs to the state of Texas."

"What isn't held by purchase," said Stuart.

Anne looked at him. "I know!" she said bitterly. "You and my husband and all the smart men in Texas who had money bought up land certificates, came up here and took up all the good land there was!"

Stuart looked away. "We only did what anybody would have done if they could."

"Miss Anne," George Nichols said gently, "we took cattle land. We haven't touched the land up on the plains."

"No, of course not." Her brown eyes flashed scornfully. "But what's happening up there now? What was bound to happen with Texas cattlemen crowding the plains? Right now," she said, "General Mackenzie and Colonel Miles and

Major Price are hunting down Indians on the plains like wolves. Would they be doing that if we hadn't moved in here next to the Caprock?"

Utah said bluntly, "Ma'am, your place is on it, too."

Anne looked at them helplessly. "That's the worst of it," she said huskily. "Will Schooler never told me what we were getting into, and now everything we have is in the ranch. We have to stay and fight or we have to give up everything."

Stuart saw that she was about to cry. "Well, ma'am—" He got up awkwardly. He would have liked to put his arms around her and comfort her, but he was too well aware that he had no right to do anything like that. "It's nothing anybody did personally," he said, trying to make it seem casual. "It's just—well, things happen that way." He realized the explanation was not very convincing, and he added, out of the confusion in his own mind, "I reckon the Indians probably chased out somebody on their own hook before we got here."

She swallowed hard, tears in her eyes. Stuart moved toward her. "There's not much any of us can do but sweat it out," he said.

George Nichols said from his chair, "You're upset, Miss Anne. One of the men will see you safe home."

Nobody else said a word. Then the sound of a galloping horse came from the hard-packed yard. Utah watched the door with cynical eyes. There was a great commotion outside. The horse backed and swung around, and the rider kept calling, "Whoa now! Whoa, you!"

Nobody went to the door.

Finally it opened, and Will Schooler came in. "I heard shootin' and Indians yellin'," he said.

Utah said sourly, "I figgered you'd be here as soon as it was over."

Will Schooler said slowly, "I don't know what you mean by that. I came as soon as I could."

Utah pulled down his hat and walked out.

Schooler started to follow him but turned back. "I don't know why everybody is so— Anne! Annie, what's the matter? You're crying!" He glared at them all. "If somebody laid a hand on her, I'll—I'll—"

Stuart said wearily, "Go dig a post hole."

"I'm tired," she said through her tears. "And I'm scared. There were Indians here, Will—Cheyennes—on the warpath. I'm scared. I want to go back home."

94

"Well," he said, "we'll certainly go home." He looked uncertainly at George Nichols. "If I had a man like Utah Thompson, I'd fire him."

George said evenly, "Maybe that's why you're always short-handed, Will."

Schooler said, "Mr. Nichols, if you think you can run my ranch better—"

"No offense, Will." George, too, sounded tired.

Anne moved toward the door. "We'd better go, Will. It's been—upsetting."

They went outside. Five of the Rocking Seven men were dragging Indian bodies away with their lariats, heading toward the flat on the northeast, near the path down which the Cheyennes had come.

George Nichols said in a low voice, "I guess you're right, what you been thinkin' without saying. She could use a shoulder to lean on. That numskull Will Schooler is about as understanding as a gate post."

Stuart nodded. "Will's twice as old as she is. I doubt he ever notices the right things about her."

"Some day he'll fool you," said George. "Some day he'll catch on to the fact that nobody has any use for him, and he'll connect that up with Anne and Anne up with somebody else—like you, for instance—and, because he is twice as old, he'll make trouble—big trouble."

Stuart turned back. "Anne wouldn't look at anybody else."

"That don't keep him from thinkin' it. Why do you suppose he keeps her in them men's clothes instead of letting her dress up in something real feminine?" His father looked at him. "You was studyin' her before you went to Fort Union and you had a strange look in your eyes. What was in your mind then?"

Stuart said slowly, "I was wondering if she had a dress— and I guess I felt kind of sorry for her, because I don't think she has." He paused. "And I was thinking that if I was Will Schooler I'd buy her dresses—a lot of dresses—pretty dresses."

His father studied him. Then he turned away.

CHAPTER XIII

STUART went outside. In the middle of the yard, Schooler had finally gotten in the saddle and was going through the usual unnecessary motions that tended only to make the horse more aware of his fear and more nervous.

Anne swung into her saddle and said, "Wait a minute, Will. I want to look at the *moro*."

"I'm already mounted," he said.

"Your horse will stand. I want to see the *moro*."

Stuart was puzzled. He'd never seen Anne like that. Usually she waited on Will hand and foot. Stuart limped across the yard toward the corral.

Anne followed him on the roan.

"How's the *moro* coming?" she asked as she rode alongside.

"Slow, according to some people's notions. Fine, according to mine."

Will Schooler said something under his breath. Then he turned his long-legged bay and walked it across the yard, jerking back unnecessarily on the reins.

Stuart lifted a rawhide loop off a post and crawled between the poles of the gate. Favoring his game leg considerably, he walked slowly toward the *moro*. It watched him for a moment, took a step toward him and then wheeled away.

"He's a beautiful horse," she said almost in a whisper.

"Have you saddled him yet?" demanded Schooler, coming up behind them.

Stuart didn't look at Schooler. "A lot of people want to tell me how to break this horse," he said, "but I've got a system of my own." He glanced at Anne. "I'm going to ride down the pasture a ways with you to see Pablo," he said, and moved to another pen. He picked a rope off a post, tossed a loop across the gray's neck and pulled the horse toward him.

Anne moved over on the roan. "I don't like the look in the gray's eyes," she said. "The men were talking that Fisher rode him back. Has anybody ridden him since?"

"No—but he's gentle."

He opened the gate, led the gray outside, closed the gate and mounted. The gray promptly snorted and began to buck, first to the southwest, then to the northwest. Stuart, who had not settled down in the saddle, didn't have a chance. He went spread-eagled in the dust.

The gray kept pitching. Stuart rolled over on his back, holding in a groan.

Anne's roan streaked in to the gray's side. She caught the bridle and pulled the horse's head back to one side. The gray quit pitching. She got the reins and led it back.

Stuart got up slowly. He could feel blood running down his leg.

"You shouldn't have tried to ride," Anne said, half scolding, half concerned.

Utah was standing at the corral, one heel up, whittling a stick with his scalping knife.

Will Schooler said, "You should have known the gray would pitch."

Whitey, a man who had the look of limber rawhide, came up from the harness-shed.

"Where you been?" asked Stuart.

Whitey said, "We choused up a black bear up in the breaks, there, and we was puttin' the iron on him when we heard the shootin'. I tried to turn the bear loose, but it got sort of complicated."

Andy chuckled. "You should of seen that b'ar, Mist' Nichols. His blood was lettin' off steam enough to beat the Robert E. Lee from New'leans to Memphis."

Stuart asked, "Any horses hurt by the bear?"

"Not ourn," said Whitey.

Stuart walked toward the house with Whitey. "You hear anything unusual up there today?"

"Shootin'," said Whitey. "But that's as common as lice on a hawk's foot."

"You never saw anything," asked Stuart, "like as if somebody might have been signaling?"

Whitey shook his head. "Can't say I did."

They stood around the grave. It wasn't very deep, because the soil was rocky. They wrapped Brisket in a worn buffalo robe and lowered him on their bridle reins. Stuart took off his hat, and Utah, Dusty, Slim and the other hands stood around, silent, and took off their hats and wiped their foreheads with their shirt sleeves.

George Nichols hadn't come; it was too far for him to walk. He stood on his crutches at the side of the house, his hat off, his white hair shining in the sun.

Pablo rode up and got off his horse. He took off his big felt hat and came up behind the others. They all stood awkwardly for a moment, nobody quite able or willing to say anything. Andy leaned against the shovel he had used to dig the grave.

Finally Stuart swallowed and stepped forward a pace. "Brisket Smith was a good hand," he said, looking up a little, his words breaking queerly against the rising wind. "He could throw a loop tighter'n a necktie at a hangin', and he could put it any place that stuck out on a critter." He stopped, self-conscious. Then, feeling that his words somehow had been inadequate, he added lamely, "He was a good hand with a trail-herd, too."

Stuart stepped back slowly. The rising wind sent little curtains of gravel sliding down into the grave.

Dusty said explosively, "He could read a brand as far as most men could tell a cow from an antelope."

Pablo talked softly in Spanish. He crossed himself and was silent.

Dusty spoke suddenly, relief apparent in his voice. "Grab that shovel, Slim."

Dusty and Slim began shoveling—unceremoniously, because there wasn't much use apologizing to a corpse for throwing dirt in his face. They all began to talk at once, not about Brisket or the Indians, but about cows and grass and horses. Stuart knew they were as relieved as he was. He put on his hat, got into the saddle slowly and carefully and rode the gray back to the harness-shed.

His father was already working on the saddle.

"It seemed like old times," said George. "Remember when the Kiowas used to raid us down on the Brazos?"

"I know," Stuart said, reaching for the dipper. "I was the one who found Mrs. Sherman."

His father looked at him, suddenly caught short. "I remember. You might' near went crazy." He said suddenly, "You changed since then, Stuart. You shot Indians today like you was doing it for money."

"They attacked us," said Stuart, and his tone indicated that he felt nothing more needed to be said. Then he added, "We'll be heading for the plains again tomorrow."

"You just got back."

"The Army will be here tomorrow," said Stuart, "and I'll want the same crew I had."

"Fisher, too?"

Stuart looked up at the Caprock. "I want him where I can watch him."

The steady chopping of Utah's adze came from the end of the shed outside. Stuart got up and walked around.

"Can you see a Cheyenne if they come up here tonight?"

Utah dropped the adze across the cottonwood log and took a chew from the pocket of his buckskin shirt. "Cain't nobody see an Injun unless the Injun wants to be seen," he said, and bit into the chew. "But I can smell 'em."

"Then you better sit up a while tonight and keep your smeller peeled."

Utah bit into the chew, twisted it off and picked up the adze again. "Too bad we lost old Ginger up on the plains. That mule was raised in Colorado, and she could smell an Injun farther'n a steer would run to water on a hot day."

Stuart went back to the house and found a good pistol. He loaded it and put it in his holster. "I could use a cup of coffee," he told the cook.

The cook studied him. "You're a mite pale. Set down for a minute and I'll warm it up."

Right then, a few minutes' rest sounded good. He sat down in the big rawhide-seated chair that his father had made when they first came to this country, in '66—though that had not been on this ranch. George had been more conservative then; they stayed farther east in the breaks.

Stuart straightened out his leg in front of him and leaned back. He closed his eyes for a minute, and the next thing he knew Dusty was talking to him. "Feller from the Army comin' up to see you, Stuart."

His father, braced on his crutches, was rinsing his face on

the wash bench outside the door. Four horses trotted into the yard, and Stuart watched the blue-uniformed riders come toward the ranch house. He went to the door.

"Major Whitehead," he said.

Whitehead smiled. "Mr. Nichols, I'm glad to see you."

They shook hands.

"This here's my father, George Nichols."

"Glad to know you, sir," said Whitehead. "Get that leg in the war?" he asked pleasantly.

"Nope, the Yankees was damn' lousy shots. I got this from a rattlesnake."

"Sorry to hear it."

"Come on in," said Stuart. "We got hot coffee."

Whitehead asked, "Where'd you get that leg wound?"

"I got that from Six Arrows. They raided the Tesecato about three hours ago."

Whitehead leaned forward. "Mr. Nichols, did it occur to you to mark the spot where you cached the lead?"

"Certainly."

"Then it would occur to others that you had done so."

"I suppose so," said Stuart.

"We now have definite evidence, Mr. Nichols, that the Cheyennes have received information from somebody, either in your party or in the Army, as to the burial of the lead."

"Such as?"

"Baldwin's scouts, on the way back to join Miles, brought in a Cheyenne prisoner—a young warrior named Gray Eagle Feather. He got in a fuss with Stone Calf over the campaign. Gray Eagle Feather wanted to go up and down the Caprock and wipe out the whites, while Stone Calf thought they'd better restrict their fighting to the Army. Anyway, his story is that Stone Calf tried to kill him, but he got away. He saw Baldwin's camp and walked into it one night. They sent him in to Fort Sill."

"Have you talked to him, Major?"

"Through an interpreter—yes. He said the Cheyennes knew a great deal about you, Mr. Nichols. They call you Many Mules."

"That's possible. I freighted to the reservation for years, and sometimes I hired some of them."

"He says Stone Calf is sure you would never leave that ton of lead in the ground without marking it."

"Then they do know it's in the ground."

"It sounds that way. And they say they can make you tell."

"They'll have to catch me first."

Whitehead looked at Stuart. He got up and went to the stove with his coffee cup, came back with it full, and stood across the table from Stuart. He said, "I understood they were going to try that today, Mr. Nichols."

CHAPTER XIV

STUART got halfway to his feet. He remembered the many perplexing aspects of the raid—its being made in daylight, almost in the shadow of U. S. troops, the many other strange things they had noted about it. Now the seeming inexplicability was clear in one flash of understanding. But it was a knowledge that left him cold and weak, because, if the raid had succeeded, he would be facing Stone Calf over a torture pit. He swallowed hard and sat down slowly. "So that's what they were up to," he said weakly.

The major said, "It must be unsettling news, but I thought you'd better be warned."

"It lets me know what to expect, anyway."

"Gray Eagle Feather says that Stone Calf has worked out a campaign by which he expects to win the war in the Panhandle—that it depends only on his getting ammunition for two days' fighting."

Stuart said, stirring the sugar in his coffee, "Glad you told me, Major."

Whitehead got up. "Can you show me the trail over the Caprock?"

"I'll send Dusty with you."

Stuart limped to the door and watched him go, Dusty leading. Then George came in. "The major musta been in a hurry."

Stuart said, "Things are moving pretty fast up there in the hills."

He walked around, exercising his leg, until the cook called out the back door, "Supper's on!"

Everybody but Utah came in. They slid onto the long benches around the big table, and everybody ate with their hats on.

They finished the meal in silence. Then, almost in concert, they got up. Stuart said, "I'll send Utah in for grub."

Stuart went out to the feed barn beyond the harness shed. Utah was sitting on a sack of oats in the shadow, watching the Caprock.

"Feed's on," said Stuart. "I'll watch a while."

Utah got up slowly and spat out his chew. "The sun throws some almighty strange shadows over there on the Caprock this time of day," he observed. "I don't think there's anything up there, but the light's a fooler."

"I'll let off a shot if I see anything," said Stuart.

He sat there and thought about it. He couldn't see any way the Indians could know so much about the lead unless somebody had told them—and that somebody had to be Fisher. . . .

Stuart posted two guards, and, as an added precaution, he slept in the harness-shed with Pablo. At midnight he woke up with his leg pretty sore, so he went up to the house and got Dusty and Whitey to take over the watch. Utah went to sleep in the shed, on a bag of corn.

Lieutenant Garner came down the north trail about noon with twelve men. He was a young man with a back like a ramrod and a very wide mustache that seemed too old for him. He said, "I hear you don't like Indians, Mr. Nichols."

Stuart asked, "Where did you hear that? Nobody likes Indians."

Garner shrugged. "It was just mentioned. When can you go with us to look for the lead?"

"In half an hour."

Stuart gave orders to Utah, Dusty, and Pablo to be ready to travel. Dusty said, "We could take the mules with us and bring back the wagons."

"There won't be any wagons left," said Stuart. "The Cheyennes have been up there."

He decided to ride to the LHJ with Garner. If he and Fisher were to be in the same party for several days, there was no sense standing at swords' point.

103

They went through the Bar M and found Will Schooler still working at his hay. Then they trotted by the Schoolers' house, and Anne, hanging out the wash, waved at them.

They went on to the LHJ and up to Fisher's house. It was a sod house, like most of those in the breaks area below the Caprock, but it needed plastering. Another five years and it would melt down.

Stuart stayed on the gray while Garner called out, "Hello."

Fisher came around from behind the house. His eyes widened when he saw Nichols and Garner, but his manner changed when Garner explained what he wanted.

"Sure, I'll go. Yes, I'll go. Why don't you men ride on back and I'll catch up to you in a little while? I've got a few errands to do before I can leave."

Garner said pleasantly, "All right. Half an hour, maybe?"

"About that."

They rode back to the Bar M, and Will Schooler came out on his long-legged bay. "I am offering my services to your party," he told Garner. "So far I haven't done anything for anybody in this Indian trouble, and I think it's time for me to help."

Stuart studied him for a moment. No doubt that he was sincere. Stuart looked at Anne. She was anxious.

Garner said, "All right with me, Mr. Schooler. The more the merrier."

Anne looked up at them, shading her eyes against the sun. "Won't you gentlemen step in and have a piece of plum pie? I baked it fresh this morning."

Garner said, "I don't mind if I do, ma'am." He got down. "We have to wait on Fisher anyway." He looked at her more closely. "A very pleasant surprise, ma'am, to find such a pretty woman out here among the Cheyennes. I daresay you're stunning in a dress."

She blushed and turned away.

Stuart glanced at Schooler. The man's face was set in hard lines.

Anne said, "Mr. Nichols, would you mind getting me a bucket of water?"

Stuart smiled. "It would be a pleasure, ma'am."

He limped down to the creek, filled the bucket carefully from one side so as not to stir up the sand in the creek bed and turned to see Anne Schooler coming toward him.

104

"I'm so sorry, Mr. Nichols," she said aloud. "I forgot about your injury."

"It's not that bad, really," he said.

In a whisper she said, "Please look after Will. You *know* how he is. He can't do anything right, and I'm *so* afraid. He has no business up there on the Llano."

He balanced the bucket of water on his knee. "Then why didn't you put your foot down?" he asked. "Or say you need him on the ranch?"

"He knows I don't need him. That's the trouble, I guess; nobody needs him at all." She said earnestly, "This means a lot to him, Mr. Nichols. You see, he doesn't have any confidence in himself as a man."

He looked down at her. "I reckon I'm not the one to say it's a strange way to try to get confidence. If it suits him, I guess it ought to suit us." He noted how her hair lay in small curls on her neck. "If I can keep him out of trouble, ma'am, I'll do it."

She pressed his hand. "Thank you," she whispered.

She preceded him up the path to the house. "Will is going to get me some chickens," she said aloud, "but we are told the coyotes are very bad."

It was a poor attempt at a covering-up conversation, but Stuart answered soberly, "Yes, ma'am, I hear they are."

He went inside and set the bucket on the wash bench. Garner was telling Will Schooler about life in Washington, D.C.

They ate Anne's pie and got up to leave. She said, "Will, please be careful."

He nodded. "Don't worry about me."

They went on to the Rocking Seven. Everybody was saddled when Fisher rode up. His mood again was as if nothing untoward had ever occurred between him and Stuart. "I see you've still got the *moro* in the breaking pen," he said.

"Haven't had time to work on him," said Stuart.

Fisher looked at the horse with a gleam in his buttermilk-blue eyes. "I'd sure like to show you how to break that horse," he said.

Stuart got up. "I always break my own horses."

They trailed up the Tesecato on the left side of the creek and followed the wagon road up the *puerta*. They walked their horses out onto the great prairie and dismounted for fifteen minutes to let the horses have a breather.

Garner asked, "What are we going to do for water for the horses?"

"There's a small spring about fifteen miles west of this spot. I suggest we camp there tonight—it's almost dark now —and tomorrow we'll head straight south. I don't think it will be over half a day's ride south, and perhaps if we're lucky we'll find the stuff tomorrow. If not, we'll camp dry and look most of the next day, then ride back to the spring at night."

"It's a hard program," said Garner.

"There's no other, up here."

They rode on to the spring. It was small, and somebody had sunk a barrel in the sand so buckets could be dipped in it. It took quite a while to water the horses, but there was plenty. And by the time the horses were taken care of, fires were going and supper was on.

They were all tired, and after supper Garner put out his guards and the rest of them turned in.

Utah said, "I don't like the way them horses are restless, but maybe it's account of the change. Maybe there's a norther comin'."

"I don't think so," Stuart said, yawning.

Utah rolled up in his blanket. "I hope I wake up with my own scalp on."

The last thing Stuart remembered was the bluish-red glow of the buffalo-chip fire. Then his eyes closed.

The next thing he knew, a hard hand was over his mouth. Strong arms held him with a grip like a steel vise, and he was propelled silently to his feet. He smelled Indian. Feeling a knife point against his back, opposite his heart, he knew better than to make a disturbance. He walked carefully, not seeing his captors in the dark, but knowing from the soft slap of buckskin thongs that all of them were Indians. A hundred yards from the camp he was lifted bodily onto a horse; he knew from the saddle that it was an Indian horse. The knife point never left his back. An Indian mounted the horse behind him, took the reins and kicked the horse into motion.

CHAPTER XV

THEY traveled for an hour without stopping. The knife was taken out of his back, and Stuart breathed a little easier. Surreptitiously he discovered that his six-gun belt was not hanging anywhere on the saddle. He had not thought it would be.

At the end of an hour they changed course to the northeast, and the Indian behind Stuart took a separate horse.

They hit the Canadian River just before dawn. Stuart's leg was hurting intensely. He got a drink, and then sat in the water to cool his aching thigh.

An Indian jerked at his shoulder. Stuart got up with a grunt. No word was spoken. He got into the saddle again, and they went east along the river. They were below the plains now, having come off the Llano by following the course of a small dry stream.

They followed the broad river bed until the sun came up, and then Stuart got a look at his captors.

They were four Cheyennes, stripped to the waist. They wore moccasins and buckskin leggings with long thrums, and they had no hair ornaments. They were armed only with bows and arrows, and they had not brought his gun-belt.

"How far we going?" asked Stuart.

His only answer was a grunt.

About mid-morning, he made out a small cavalry patrol coming toward them from the east. For a moment he was hopeful, but the Cheyennes had seen it, too. They rode quietly up a small draw and into a plum thicket. They dismounted. For a moment Stuart was hopeful they had been seen, but then he realized the Indian paint ponies blended easily into the background of sand and rocks. Also, since the Indians had not been riding out in the middle of the river bed but along the edge, they had the advantage of vegetation and broken contours.

He was still hopeful that the patrol would spot the Indians before they passed, but the Cheyennes held the horses down on their sides and clamped their brown fingers over the muzzles. Stuart watched their preoccupation with still more hope, but a moment later he felt the knife point in his back and heard a grunt from one of the Cheyennes. He turned his head and saw a big fourteen-inch bowie knife at his back. A young Cheyenne warrior was holding the knife with one hand and a horse's muzzle with the other. Stuart took a look at the warrior's face and decided not to commit suicide by making a sound.

His hopes sank as the patrol rode on by. A quarter of an hour later they were out of sight. The big bowie knife dropped away from his back, and the Cheyennes let their horses up. They mounted and rode on east, and half an hour later they turned into a small ravine and rode south.

Six miles from the river, at about noon, they rode through a narrow pass in the rocks and came suddenly upon a large Indian village.

Stuart guessed there were about two hundred tepees. His captors led him through the twisting paths and stopped in front of one tepee that was highly painted and decorated in many colors. There was some conversation as they dismounted. A squaw came out of the tepee and talked to them, then went back inside. The Indians dismounted, and Stuart got down and stretched his leg. Some of the soreness was out of it, but there was a dull throbbing that would stay, he knew, until he got some rest.

The squaw built a fire of cottonwood branches under a brass kettle. She brought water and half filled the kettle. Then she took a piece of meat that looked like the haunch of an antelope, cut it up and dropped it into the water.

The Indians who had captured him squatted around the fire.

Stuart remained standing, flexing his knee to keep his leg from getting stiff. Presently one of the Indians noticed his movements and looked at him. He saw the blood on Stuart's leg, pointed and said, "Ma-he."

The others gathered around and seemed to be asking the

young Indian if he had done it with the knife. The Cheyenne shook his head.

Stuart called on what little Cheyenne he knew. *"Mi-otze, navone, naguth.* An arrow—two days ago."

This brought another discussion in Cheyenne among the four.

Stuart struggled with his scanty memory of Cheyenne words. Finally he said, *"Mah-pa, o-esth,"* which he hoped would mean hot water.

The oldest one nodded. His name, as near as Stuart could understand it, was Buffalo Tail. He went into a long discussion with the other three, and then with the squaw. Eventually she brought another kettle filled with water and put it in the fire.

Stuart felt relieved. Apparently it was not a part of their immediate program to let him die of the wound.

The squaw shuffled around and put on coffee. The four Indians produced a sack of tobacco and some papers, with which they began to make cigarettes. Buffalo Tail turned abruptly to Stuart and said, *"Sin-na-mon."*

Stuart nodded. They gave him the sack and the papers.

Meantime, the area in front of the tent and the fire around which they sat had become the center of attention for a large group of Indians of all ages, but mostly women and children. A few old men were there but no warriors, and Stuart realized that this camp was almost defenseless. The Indians stood silently, their great black eyes focused on Stuart, but he got more a feeling of curiosity than hostility.

After another hour, a single horseman galloped into the other end of camp and slowed down to a trot as he came toward the fire, where the coffee was boiling and the meat simmering.

The rider slid off the horse, and a boy about ten years old ran forward to take the *mecate.*

The men sitting at the fire continued to sit but watched the newcomer. He was a big Indian who looked intelligent and had a competent and sharp manner. His quick eyes seemed to take in everything. His face was lined with weariness and worry. He stood in front of Stuart and said, "You —Nichols? Cheyenne call Many Mules?"

Stuart nodded.

The big Indian put a finger on his chest. "White men call me Stone Calf. I am chief of Southern Cheyennes."

Stuart nodded. "Stone Calf's name is well known among all persons in Texas."

Stone Calf went into his lodge, and the others resumed smoking.

After a while, the squaw brought out a couple of tin plates and put the meat in them. Buffalo Tail motioned to Stuart to help himself, and cut a large chunk for him. Stuart took it in his fingers.

Stone Calf came and ate with them, and after a few moments the meat was cleaned up and the coffee—which was very thin—was gone. Stone Calf sat back and regarded Nichols without any apparent emotion.

"For many hundreds of years," he said, "the Indian owned this great prairie, these canyons, these many rivers, the buffalo and antelope upon them. For many hundreds of years, our forefathers lived well and happily. There were wars between tribes, but those were settled in the Indian fashion, and there was always plenty of prairie, much buffalo for all. No matter who won the fight, there was food and clothing for the defeated." He looked into the distance. "Then the white man came. He had better weapons, and he came in great numbers, like the buffalo. There was no way to avoid him. He tangled with our warriors. It was no more the fault of one than of the other, but the Indian always paid through the ground he was forced to give up—ground that he had used long before the white man brought his horses across the big water." He paused.

"The white man made promises. First he gave worthless presents, and then whisky, and each time the Indian had to give up more land and move somewhere else so the white man could drive his stakes and pull his plows and build his houses. And each time the white man promised that the new boundaries would be held sacred forever."

He paused a long time, seemingly lost in thought. The four Cheyennes around the fire looked into the coals, and the ring of spectators remained silent. Finally Stone Calf began again.

" 'Forever' does not seem to mean the same thing to the white man as it does to the Indian. 'Forever' to the white man means until he wants more. Then the stake-drivers come west and the farmers follow behind with their plows, and the railroads are built, and the buffalo are killed, and

110

the Indian is put on a reservation. The Cheyennes are moved from the Black Hills, which was our forefathers' hunting ground, to barren land in the Indian Territory, where there is little game. The white man, to make sure the Indian will know the gnawing hunger at his bowels, will not let him have powder and lead, and he must get a pass from the superintendent to look for the few buffalo that are left. Even with the pass, he may be killed by the soldiers if he is found with a rifle in his hands, though he has no intention of harming anybody but is merely trying to get meat for his hungry wives and children."

Stuart moved a little to ease his leg. He didn't know how long this would go on.

"Then," said Stone Calf, "some of our tribes who valued freedom more than life determined to wage a great war for possession of the plains and the buffalo. It always was our land and it is not now for the *Tejanos* to claim it and use it and to kill the buffalo on it and let them rot in the summer sun.

"So we broke out of the reservations. Many stayed behind —those of weak hearts who did not think we could defeat the great masses of white soldiers, or those who were satisfied to stay in the villages and raise corn and pumpkins and report to the agent every thirty days for food given in charity or not given at all." His voice was filled with scorn.

"And so a great number of us took our few possessions and our wives and children and came to fight for the land that was ours in the beginning." He looked up. "Now the Great White Father has sent many armies of soldiers against us to drive us back to the reservations, but they have reckoned without the pride of heritage of the Cheyenne and the Arapaho and the Kiowa and the Comanche. These are many, and the plains are our natural home, and none can fight better on them than we. The white generals know this, and Mackenzie and Miles know that we are very near to winning this war for our rightful heritage, and they are making every effort to prevent it." He studied Stuart.

"Your white men and your white soldiers have killed and murdered Cheyenne women and children. They have slaughtered and burned whole villages."

Stuart said, "Your Indian warriors have done the same. I have seen it."

"I am not excusing the Cheyennes, but I think of the

111

village of Red Turtle near which you and one of your men rode three days ago. This village was of women and children and old men, but the brave soldiers of the white general charged them again and again, shot them and pierced them with sabers and finally exterminated them like dogs."

Stuart asked, "How do you know I went by this village?"

"We see many things," said Stone Calf. "We are not always killing and scalping as some of your people say. Now we know that you brought back across the plains a wagonload of lead. We captured the gunpowder but it is useless without lead for bullets. And with bullets enough for all my warriors we can surround the white soldiers and drive them back into the Territory—where perhaps they can raise their own corn and pumpkins and report to the Indian agent every thirty days for a beggar's gift of coffee and tobacco." He looked up, suddenly fierce. "There are some of us who do not like having to plead for subsistence."

"Did Fisher tell you about the lead?" asked Stuart.

Stone Calf looked down. "We have many ways of knowing what happens."

"But you have no way of knowing where I buried the lead."

Stone Calf sounded tired. "The great wind has erased every trace." He looked keenly at Stuart. "But we know that you can find it. That is why you went up on the plains with the soldiers."

"But I haven't told anybody else, and I'm not going to tell you."

Stone Calf said patiently, "I have tried to show you that we Cheyennes are fighting only for what is ours. I know that sometimes our young braves—and sometimes older ones who should know better—have raided and killed white settlements, but our people have always done that. We cannot learn better in one generation. We have always done it with other Indians, and they have raided back, but there have been no great wars of extermination like this one your white generals are forcing upon us."

"But—"

"It was to be expected when whites moved in on our hunting grounds, and those whites knew it. But they have moved in anyway, and now they cry because the very thing happens that they expected to happen, while the Cheyennes cry because their children go hungry and their wives have no buffalo robes to make tepees when the old ones fall to pieces under the sun and rain."

"So the whole story is that you want me to show you where the lead is," Stuart said bluntly.

Stone Calf looked at him with his deep, sad eyes. "I have hoped you would understand."

Stuart shook his head firmly. "I will have no part of furnishing lead to Indians to kill whites."

"I am prepared," Stone Calf said imperturbably, "to offer you a choice. You may have the same reward I promised Fisher."

"What is that?"

"That when the Indians once again control the Texas Panhandle, we will allow you to remain in the Tesecato and run your ranch as you are now running it."

Stuart stared at the Cheyenne. Stone Calf had come into the open with his mention of Fisher. But the proof that Fisher was working with the Indians was not the most significant aspect of Stone Calf's offer. Nor was it the fact that Fisher did expect to keep his land if the Indians won. The most important fact of the moment was that Stone Calf had told him about it. That meant that Stone Calf did not expect him to return to his ranch alive unless they made a deal.

Stuart, working for time to think, said at last, "You do expect to win, don't you?"

"We do," said Stone Calf. "And I will tell you why." He went into his tent and came back with half a dozen black-haired scalps. "You know what these are, Nichols?"

"They're scalps."

"How old, do you think?"

"Three or four days."

"This one?"

Stuart nodded slowly. The hair was gray.

"And these two are from small children."

"The squaws must have been fighting back."

"When you see the great white general, ask him how many of these squaws in Red Turtle's village were found shot in the back as they were running—some as far away as a quarter of a mile from the village." Stone Calf's eyes blazed. "Does this sound like squaws shooting at soldiers?"

Stuart eyed the scalps silently.

"And ask your general how many children were found shot in the back. Children of three and four summers." His

113

lip curled scornfully. "Is this the valor of the white soldier?"

"It's war," said Stuart.

Stone Calf whipped out one more—a peculiar-looking scalp shaped like a black mustache. "White man, look on this! It was taken from between the legs of a Cheyenne woman!" His eyes blazed, and the four around the fire grunted wrathfully.

Stuart drew a deep breath.

"Is this war, too?" asked Stone Calf.

"It is unnecessary," said Stuart.

"Both sides do unnecessary things. We know that. But I say both sides. Not the Indians alone. You know that, Nichols?"

Stuart nodded.

"We fight for our lives, for our honor, for our dignity. Is there any better thing to fight for?"

Stuart said, "I'm a white man. You can't expect me to help you kill my own kind, even when some of the white men kill women and children."

"White!" Stone Calf's voice was filled with derision. "What kind of skin means what, Nichols? Are there not good men and bad men of both colors? You think of Indians as bad, but I tell you today there are white men we would not allow to live in a Cheyenne tribe."

Stuart said, "Yes, including the man Fisher."

Stone Calf's face was unmoved. "You whites have a saying about looking a gift horse in the mouth."

Stuart said, "All this makes no difference. I'm not a man like Fisher, and I will not show you where the lead is."

Stone Calf smoked a long time in silence. Finally he talked in Cheyenne to the other four. Then he turned to Stuart. "I give you until midnight. If you do not agree to show us then, we will make you do it."

Stuart swallowed. There was no mistaking the determination in the chief's face. "Even if I showed you, the cavalry is up there."

Stone Calf snorted. "Cavalry! My warriors can whip them one against two! We are going to fight differently now, Nichols. We are going to fight the white man's way. We have learned to charge in fearlessly. We know that a few may die so that others will live. We will take all the ammunition we have and wipe out the cavalry and dig up the lead."

"How will you get it out of the ground?"

Stone Calf said, "I am thinking about that now."

"I will have to consider," Stuart said finally.

"You have until midnight," Stone Calf repeated.

Stuart said, "I'd like to know something. If those scalps were taken by white soldiers, how did you get them?"

Stone Calf looked coldly at him. "You doubt my word! You force my greatest shame! My own daughter was among the Cheyennes at the village." His eyes blazed. "She was twelve years old, and she was the only one taken alive. The white soldiers took her alive and violated her repeatedly, and later she recovered these scalps and found her way to Gray Beard's camp, where she told me what had happened."

"I would like to talk to her for myself," said Stuart after a moment.

Stone Calf's eyes looked watery. "Nichols, you may have an opportunity to do that in the great hunting ground. For, after her brutal treatment by the soldiers and her flight on foot through forty miles of hilly country, she did not live but a few hours. You have said war causes many sad things, Nichols. I wonder if you know anything sadder than this!"

CHAPTER XVI

STONE CALF's last words made for some pretty serious thought. Such conduct was not condoned by the higher officers, and Stuart had not the slightest doubt that if it came to light the perpetrators would be court-martialed. But how did you explain the difference between a few Kiowas on the Brazos and a few whites on Whitefish Creek who did the same thing?

Stone Calf said to the warriors, "Many Mules will not be tied." He looked at Stuart. "The village is filled with women and old men who will swarm on you with knives if you try to get away."

Stuart said, "With this leg I couldn't get far, anyway."

Stone Calf considered. "I will get a doctor for you."

Stuart said, "Why get a doctor when you're going to kill me tonight anyway?"

Stone Calf looked at him. Stone Calf was a man of average height, but was very thick and solid in the body and powerful in the arms and legs. He had a broad nose and wide mouth, which seemed frequently to be about to smile, but when Stuart looked at the Cheyenne's narrowed eyes he knew it was not a smile. Deep lines extended from the corners of Stone Calf's mouth to the sides of his nose to give him an air of doing things that he might not want or like to do—but there could be no doubt, after a glance at those unswerving eyes, that he would do whatever needed doing. And now he turned his eyes on Stuart and said briefly, "We're not going to kill you. We're going to make you tell us how to find the lead."

A wrinkled old Indian, Broken Antelope Horn, almost black from countless summers under the western sun, came up. He could talk no English, but Stone Calf told him to look at Stuart's leg. The old Indian looked at Stuart. *"Mi-otze?"* he asked.

Stuart nodded.

Broken Antelope Horn talked to Stone Calf, and Stone Calf said to Stuart, "He says you are in no danger. It is an angry wound but he has medicine for it."

"Mah-e-tse-i-yo," said the old Cheyenne.

"It is a medicine used to stop bleeding and cool the skin," said Stone Calf. "He will go to his lodge and prepare it."

The old doctor came back. He ripped off the green cloth; Stuart saw that it was soaked with blood and that fresh blood was oozing out of the wound. The old man produced a small buckskin sack and sprinkled some kind of dusty powder over the wound. He held it in place with leaves while Stuart turned over and had the other side treated the same way. The old man bound it all with a strip torn from a white man's shirt. Then he closed his eyes and mumbled in Cheyenne, and finally took some powder from a different bag and scattered it to the east, south, west, and north, each time chanting the same words. Then he stood up and nodded.

"You will not lose your leg," said Stone Calf.

Stuart, pulling on his trousers, was startled. He had not thought about losing it. He looked at Broken Antelope Horn and said, "Thank you."

The old man nodded, satisfied.

An attractive young Cheyenne woman came up. "I have learned to talk your language at the reservation schools." She smiled. "I used to watch you drive your many mules into Fort Sill when I was a little girl."

He said, "You aren't over eighteen now."

"I am grown," she said. "I have three children. My husband was killed in this war."

"If your husband is dead, why don't you go back to the reservation?"

She said, "My people are here. Here we do not have to beg for food and here we do not starve."

"Didn't you get food at Fort Sill?" he asked.

"In three months," she told him, "we had five pounds of cornmeal, no coffee, no sugar, one quarter of an antelope we were allowed to kill. My babies were thin, their ribs

117

like a bony horse." She shook her head sadly. "The agents were supposed to give us food, but somehow it never got there. And we have not learned to farm. We have tried it, but our men have always been hunters. It will take a long time to raise squash and pumpkins for a living. Our men want meat. They get sick if they do not have meat."

He got up on one elbow. "You are supposed to have a certain number of pounds of beef a week."

She drew herself up haughtily. "No Indian in Indian Territory has ever had *one* pound a week—and we have had to beg for that." Her black eyes flashed. "If the Indians came along and took your cattle, Many Mules, and then said to you, 'You can have one piece of meat a day,' and then you had to go every day to the agency and beg us for your piece of meat, and most of the time you did not get it anyway, do you think you would like that?"

"It's not the same thing," he said. "I've paid for those cows with money and with work."

She said, "You paid the state of Texas for your land?"

"Of course."

"You could not just go out and say 'I want this valley of the Tesecato' and build a house there and live there without paying?"

"Of course not."

"You have to buy it from Texas because Texas owns the land."

He nodded. He wondered why she was so insistent.

"Then where did Texas buy the land?"

"They—"

He stopped. What he had started to say didn't sound very good.

"Who had that land before Texas?"

"Nobody that I know of."

"I think," she said, "you know the Indians had it for many hundreds of years. You are not that ignorant, Many Mules—nor am I."

"They didn't teach you that at the agency school!"

"No, but they taught us to read and to think in the white man's thoughts. Our men are wise, Many Mules. We know this is our land by right, and we are going to make it so by force, for the white man respects nothing but force."

"What is your name?" he asked, trying to change the discussion.

"Cottonwood Leaf."

He said, "One thing, Cottonwood Leaf. If you stay out here, you may all get killed—and in the end you'll have to go back to the reservation, anyway, if any are left alive."

She smiled patronizingly. "We are not going back. We have come to the Llano to stay."

"But the soldiers?"

"Stone Calf is a wise and fearless chief, and he has learned many things from the white soldiers. He has promised us that before the buttercups bloom next spring we will have a new treaty of peace with Washington, and the Texas Panhandle will belong to the Indians, for we are going to catch the soldiers in one trap after another and massacre them as fast as they come into the Panhandle."

"Providing," he said, "I tell you where to get the lead for your bullets."

He did not like her smile when she answered. "You will tell, Many Mules, or you will lose your tongue, piece by piece."

CHAPTER XVII

Two warriors galloped into camp on fine horses and came to a plunging stop before Stone Calf's tepee, which was not over a hundred feet from Stuart. There was excited talk when Stone Calf came out, and the word *is-see-vone* was repeated a number of times. Stone Calf issued orders, and presently a dozen squaws, mounted on poorer horses, set off at a gallop toward the west rim of the valley.

Cottonwood Leaf had gone to watch, and now she came back and began to dig a hole with an elkhorn digging stick. "Two of the men have killed a buffalo," she told Stuart, "and the women have gone to butcher it. We will have meat tonight." Then she added, "I have no husband to kill meat for me, so I will cook for some of those who go to butcher."

He asked curiously, "Your husband—where was he killed, exactly?"

She straightened up, and the fire in her eyes frightened him for a moment. "My husband was Six Arrows," she said, "and he was killed when they tried to capture you two days ago. You shot him on your ranch."

Stuart was taken aback. "I didn't know him from any other," he said, "and I was defending myself."

She stopped digging. The pit was two feet square and two feet deep. On her knees, she began to line the sides with stones.

"I know," she said. "To you he was an enemy. If I thought your killing him meant anything else, I would cut your throat before you could stand up."

120

He began to think the best thing to do with Cottonwood Leaf was to keep still.

She went off toward the other end of the village. Two small boys, both naked and brown, came around from behind the tepee and yelled, *"Vee-a-ho!* White man!" and pointed their fingers at him and made noises like the explosion of a rifle.

Stone Calf had gone somewhere on his horse, and his squaw took the brass kettle down to the creek, filled it and brought it back to hang over the fire, which she built up with cottonwood sticks and a few pieces of mesquite.

Stuart got up to walk around. He thought his leg was not quite as sore as it had been.

Behind the tepee about fifty feet he saw another squaw working over a buffalo hide. It was staked out on a flat place on the ground, and apparently she had just finished fleshing it, for she was on her knees washing it with a bucket of water in which she had mashed up a large hatful of soapweed roots. She had a piece of tin cut from a tin can, and was working the soapy water into the hide, at the same time watching for bits of flesh that had not been removed.

The whole thing gave him a start, for this was not the work of a war camp or a temporary camp of any sort. It was the kind of work usually done in a camp the Indians expected to be permanent.

After a while the valley was dark, although there was still evidence of light on the western horizon. He noted that the entire village seemed occupied in wailing and mourning, so he got up and walked around the front of the tepee a while to limber up his leg, which felt considerably better. He noted that Cottonwood Leaf sat silent and motionless with her own thoughts.

A warrior galloped past on a horse. He slid off the horse at Stone Calf's tent. The new arrival called out, and Stone Calf said something from inside the lodge. The new man bent down, looked into the opening and spoke. Stone Calf answered. Then the messenger jumped on his horse and galloped back to the south.

Cottonwood Leaf got up. "You will go now to the tepee of Stone Calf," she said.

"What does it mean?" he asked, getting up.

"Go on."

He stopped outside Stone Calf's tepee. There was a fire in the fire pit, but it contained only glowing embers, no real flame. Stone Calf said, "Come in, Many Mules."

He stooped and went in, careful not to move too far, knowing that he must not go to the wrong side, he must not walk between anybody else and the fire—for now he saw, in the red glow of the embers, two other warriors besides Stone Calf—one ancient, one young. Stone Calf pointed and said, "Sit there."

He sat down, facing Stone Calf.

"We have known you a long time, Many Mules, and we have never known you to be dishonest. You are one of the few white men who talks with a straight tongue, and so you may sit with us for a moment, for we want to watch your face when you see what is about to happen."

Stuart felt a sudden choking feeling. He looked at Stone Calf's wide face and the narrowed eyes that glinted in the light of the embers. It came to him that there was nothing evil in the face—only great determination and ability, and a coldness that would enable him to do whatever had to be done. Stuart sat stiffly, waiting.

He heard horses approaching at a trot, and he judged there to be half a dozen of them. They came to the tepee and stopped. Stone Calf sat, imperturbable, unmoving.

A warrior looked into the tepee and glanced at all the faces inside. He disappeared, and a moment later the tent opening was torn aside. A figure was thrust inside, and fell sprawling on the floor of the tepee.

Startled by the abruptness of the movement, Stuart stared. Slowly he made out in the dimness of the tepee the sprawled figure—brown wool pants, a red shirt, shapeless black hat—and then in a moment the separate parts all took shape in his mind as a meaningful whole, bringing recognition just as the figure moved and lifted a white, badly scratched face toward Stone Calf.

Stuart tried to speak, but his throat was paralyzed. In another moment, he was on his feet.

"Anne!" he cried, and caught her as she rose stumbling toward him.

CHAPTER XVIII

HE held her in his arms for an instant before a warrior spun her away and left her standing, pitifully small as she faced the savages, her back against the dew cloth.

Stone Calf said, without a change of expression, "In case you prove too stubborn for us, Many Mules, I gave my warriors orders to bring this white woman, for we know that you are in love with her and you would not want her to be turned over to my warriors."

Stuart was startled. "How do you know anything like that?"

"The same way we knew that you had marked the place where you melted the lead."

Stuart stared at him. How did Stone Calf know that Gray Eagle Feather had told Miles about Fisher? "The same way," he repeated. "And that is responsible for her being brought here too?"

Stone Calf shrugged.

Stuart advanced on him. "You filthy, savage, stinking—"

Again he felt a knife in his back. This time it was Big Knife, who had come up from the shadows of the tepee. Stuart moved no further.

Stone Calf said, unmoved, "The treatment of captive women is our custom. It happens to be a custom that particularly enrages whites, just as some of your customs enrage us. But it seems to me it is more harmless than most of yours. We take nothing. She is the same when we get through with her."

Stuart was enraged. "You—" He remembered the knife.

123

"Your Cheyenne women are supposed to be noted for their chastity!" he said.

Stone Calf glanced at Anne. "She is not a Cheyenne," he observed. "She is beautiful and she is strong. In time she might make a Cheyenne squaw, but captive women have no rights until they earn them."

"You red-skinned savage!" said Anne in a low voice. "You'll never make me a squaw!"

Stone Calf regarded her through his slit eyes. "Squaws do not speak until spoken to in a Cheyenne camp," he said. "You will have to learn that."

"Wait a minute!" said Stuart. "If I lead you to the lead cache, you will turn her loose?"

Stone Calf looked at him. "Many Mules is a man of great perception."

"I'll tell," Stuart said without hesitation.

"No!" cried Anne. She looked at Stuart. "Wait, Stuart. Is this why you've always hated Indians?"

"Isn't it reason enough?"

"It's not the end of the world, Stuart."

"You don't understand," he said. "It's not just once. It's for months—if you live."

She looked at the floor and shuddered.

"Some women won't go back to civilization because of the shame," he said. "Some have gone crazy after being released. It is a terrible experience."

"But Stuart, that means showing them where you hid the lead on the Llano."

"It's nothing," he said, "compared to what they will do to you."

She faced Stone Calf. "If you get the lead, you will make bullets to stay on the warpath and to raid and maybe to capture a hundred white women and put them through the same ordeal!" She turned back to Stuart. "Where does it all end? Somebody has to sacrifice to stop it." She took a step toward Stone Calf. "We'll stop you!" she said. "You and all your kind!"

The warrior at the door shoved her brutally. She landed sprawling in front of Stone Calf, and Stuart held his breath. This was dangerous. Any display of violence would turn the Cheyennes' attention toward her as a woman. The two seemed always to go together.

Anne got slowly to her feet.

"Cheyenne women keep mouth shut," Stone Calf said coldly, "You have things to say, you talk to Many Mules—not to me. I will tell you when to talk to me."

Stuart said, fighting to keep his voice calm, "Go back to where you were. Do as he says, Anne. Please!"

She sensed the urgency in his voice and walked back to her place near the door.

Stone Calf said shrewdly, "He has not told you what may happen to him if he does not agree to show us the lead."

He shook his head, watching her with concern. "It's you I'm worried about, Anne."

She said in a low voice, "You have no right to think of me that way, Stuart." But her eyes were on his.

"I've been in love with you for a long time," he said.

Presently she said, "I—I like you, Stuart." She smiled slightly. "I always called you Mr. Nichols."

He smiled wryly. "I guess we both forgot—this time."

She straightened. "Whatever we feel, Stuart, cannot influence what we do here. I am married to Will, and I expect to stay married to him. He has treated me well—as well as he knew." Her voice broke. "Will was older. He never knew—many things. He didn't know that a woman likes—pretty clothes."

Stuart took a deep breath.

Stone Calf observed, "I seem to have given you both something to think about."

Stuart looked at him angrily. "I will promise you this, you Cheyenne savage—I am going to get out of here, and, when I do, I am going after the man who is responsible for her being here. When I get through with him he will wish the Cheyennes had him instead of me."

Stone Calf said, "You are impulsive, Many Mules. You feel very angry now, but a few days later you will be calm. It is the white man's nature. The Cheyenne—he doesn't get excited. He knows all the bad things that can happen and he expects them, and so he is not torn apart in the head when they happen. He has lived with these things too many generations, while the white man, used to all the easy comforts, comes into a violent and savage country and expects it to be like him. When a white man is like the country, then you call him an outlaw." He looked around at the Cheyennes. "White men are hard to understand."

Their faces remained impassive. Probably they did not

125

know what he was saying, although many of the Cheyennes understood English fairly well. Whatever they knew, their faces remained impassive.

Stone Calf fixed his slitted eyes on Stuart. "Remember one thing, Many Mules—we want that lead, and you know where it is. I do not know how you can find it, for my warriors have searched the plains like hawks without finding it."

"I *don't* know where it is," said Stuart, hoping to make the chief believe it.

"And yet you told Bear Coat that you could find it."

Stuart asked sharply, "How do you know that?"

Stone Calf said calmly, "There are Indian scouts with Bear Coat and with Mángomhéñte and with all the white chiefs—and among those scouts are some who have not forgotten what it is like to live in a land where the buffalo run and the antelope can be taken when Indian children are hungry. There are some who are not coffee-coolers—treaty-signers—and who do what they can to help us while the soldiers keep rifles in their backs." He watched Stuart's expression. "We have more help than you may think, Many Mules—and we are going to win. The Panhandle will belong to the Indians! This I swear!"

It was hard to face such vitality and determination. Stuart waited a moment. Then he said, "I think perhaps I understand a little better, Stone Calf, but I tell you this: I am no traitor like the one who told you I knew about the lead. I, too, have loyalty, the same as your people. As long as it is white against Cheyenne, you can not expect me to go against my own race."

Stone Calf said confidently, "I expect you to—after midnight." He looked coldly at Anne. "My warriors can use her." But he shook his head slowly. "She is dressed like no woman I have ever seen, but I don't think this will make any difference to my men."

Anne turned white, and the scratches on her face were livid. Stuart looked around and saw Big Knife laughing silently. He said angrily to Stone Calf, "You have no right to ridicule her. It is not her fault—the way she is dressed."

Stone Calf looked momentarily amused. "Nor is it ours."

Stuart said, "It is not fitting that a great chief should amuse his warriors at the expense of a woman who is helpless."

"You are prisoners," said Stone Calf. "We will do what we like with you."

"You spoke of dignity when you were on the reservation. The whites, too, have pride, and it is beneath your station to make fun of her personal appearance."

"I remind you—you are prisoners. We were not."

Stuart looked at Big Knife, who was still making a great show of laughing. Stuart would have liked to strangle him. But he turned to Anne. "Pay no attention. They're savages, just as we always thought."

"We are Cheyennes," said Stone Calf. "Our ways are not your ways, nor are your ways ours—but in such small details, Many Mules. You object to laughing at the ugly dress of this woman, but you did not object to the white soldiers who shot squaws in the back at Red Turtle's village."

For a moment Stuart had no answer, for what Stone Calf said was true. But he looked at Anne and felt doubly sorry for her. There were tears in her eyes, and he knew that even in the face of torture and ravishment she was hurt over the reference to her unwomanly appearance. He said coldly to Stone Calf, "Does the great chief rejoice that he has made a woman cry?"

Stone Calf, unperturbed, said, "Cheyenne women cry only at a death."

Stuart said bitterly, "If I ever have the chance, Stone Calf—"

The narrowed eyes did not change. Stone Calf motioned, and two of the warriors grabbed Stuart by the arms. Two more seized Anne, and they were pushed out of the lodge toward Cottonwood Leaf's tepee.

CHAPTER XIX

"It is very strange, sitting here at the door of my tepee and knowing that my husband will not return," Cottonwood Leaf said. "Many times have I sat like this and waited for him to come back out of the dark from a raid or from fighting white soldiers, and once from fighting the buffalo-wool soldiers, but always he came back, and nearly always he brought scalps. Then he would go hunting and we would have meat and buffalo skins for the tepee, and deer skins for clothing. But now," she said, "Six Arrows will come no more. I will sit here in my tepee and watch the warriors return, but Six Arrows will not be among them. And I will have to depend on the chief to allot me enough meat for myself and my children. This he will do because it is his duty, and he would be a poor chief if he did not care for his people—but it is better to have a husband of your own and somebody warm to sleep next to you on a cold night."

Anne said nothing.

There was a soft step behind Stuart, so close it startled him. There were more words in Cheyenne, and then the newcomer went away.

Cottonwood Leaf whispered, "Soldiers with the Lieutenant Garner."

"Garner?"

"Yes. They were scolded by Bear Coat for letting you get away, and now they are looking for you."

Stuart said, "I could shout."

"You will be quiet. All fires in the village are covered. All dogs are muzzled. There must be no betrayal." She moved slightly, and again he felt the knife in his side. "If you call out, Many Mules, you will die, and this squaw of the white man's pants—" She spoke derisively—"will be turned over to the Cheyenne warriors."

Anne said in a low voice, "I hear them."

"Quiet!" said Cottonwood Leaf.

The village in the small valley was in darkness. And suddenly a silence as complete as that of the very wilderness itself unfolded and settled over the village, and sounds that Stuart had not heard previously came out—crickets, frogs, a hoot owl.

A very strange feeling came over Stuart. He knew there were several hundred Cheyennes in the valley, and yet, like a single wave of complete obliteration, it was as though there was nobody in the village but him.

For a moment the strange feeling made his skin prickle. Then he shook himself and looked around to reassure himself that the dark shadows of the tepees were still against the sky. Was this a way of making war that the whites knew nothing about? Were the Cheyennes so able to concentrate on a thought that they could induce the idea in the minds of white men that nobody was there?

As he pondered this, he suddenly heard the creak of saddle leather, the slapping of leather saddle skirts and carbine boots, and a faint jingle of spur chains.

He wondered what the Cheyennes had done about their own horses to keep them from whinnying, and he concluded that some time ago they must have tied each horse's mouth with a piece of rawhide until the Army animals got past.

The party came closer, traveling on the west rim, and Stuart felt the thud of the horses' shod hoofs. A voice floated into the valley: "Sure black down there. Looks like a canyon."

"That's nothing," said another. "Everything in Texas is either a canyon or a prairie. If the general asks me, I will recommend they give it back to the Indians—and good riddance."

"The general ain't liable to ast you," said a soft Southern voice that sounded like the boy from Georgia.

"I was just iffin'."

The lieutenant spoke. He sounded tired. "The general asks the War Department about those things."

"And the War Department asks the Indian Bureau," said a new voice.

"And we follow orders," said the lieutenant.

They rode for a moment in silence. Then the Georgia boy said, "Lieutenant, sir, I hear frogs croakin'. That means water—and we ain't had no water all day. I'm dry."

"There wouldn't be any water down there."

"Sir," said another voice, "why couldn't we just light a bunch of grass and toss it over and see what it looks like down there?"

Stuart held his breath. The detail was very close to death just then.

Finally, the lieutenant answered: "Our orders are not to show a light unless absolutely necessary. If there were any Cheyennes within ten miles, we'd have a fight on our hands."

"Yes, sir."

"Anyway, we'll hit the Canadian a few miles farther north."

"Yes, sir. Do we eat then, sir?"

"We'll camp for the night, I think."

They rode along the rim. The village was utterly silent, and Stuart held his breath for what seemed like a long time. He knew the detail was surrounded by warriors, and an untoward move would have brought war arrows by the dozen. But the troops passed by and kept on north, and finally Cottonwood Leaf said, in a low voice, "They are out of hearing now. They will live for a little while longer."

Stuart tried to relax, but the feel of death was in the air, and he found his stomach pressing up in his chest.

Anne said, "What would have happened if they had discovered the village?"

"They would have been instantly killed and their bodies taken somewhere else—up on the Canadian River, perhaps. Any place where there are no Indians."

Stuart asked, "How long has the village been here in this one place?"

She answered, "Since we left the reservation, in the fat moon."

"And the soldiers have not discovered you?"

"Small parties only."

"And those—"

"Were killed, of course." She said it casually.

Big Knife said something else. She got up in the darkness them, "The soldiers are going on to the river. It is safe now."

Big Knife said something else. She got up in the darkness and stepped past Stuart. He felt the animal warmth of her body for an instant, and smelled a fragrance as of musty hay. Then she and Big Knife stood twenty feet away, talking in low voices.

"I think they're courting," said Stuart.

Anne said, "With death and killing everywhere—"

"Life goes on," he said. "Cottonwood Leaf has no husband, but she does have three children to feed. She is young and will make a good wife. And, from the looks of Big Knife, with those scars on his shoulder blades where he has swung from the pole, I would say he will be a good provider—if he lives."

"What do you mean, 'if he lives'?"

"Anne." He reached toward her in the dark and touched her arm. "This is a time when men and women don't know how long they will be on this earth. You and I both may be dead by sunrise—or maybe those soldiers were smarter than the Cheyennes think. Maybe they knew the village was here and pretended ignorance to save their own lives, and maybe Miles or Price or Mackenzie or Davidson will fall on the village at sunrise and massacre the entire band."

She asked breathlessly, "Do you really think so?"

"I do not. I am beginning to doubt, along with a lot of others, whether we will ever whip these people."

"What is to happen to us—you and me?"

"I don't know. Midnight will be here in a couple of hours, and— I don't know."

"I don't understand why he let us be together."

"Stone Calf is no ignorant savage. He wants us together so we can talk it over and I will decide to help them find the cache to save you from the warriors."

Her arm was suddenly on his shoulder, tight. "Stuart, you must not do that for me!"

"I can't do anything else."

She said tensely, "Stuart, I'm not afraid to die, if they— Stuart, I can't stand pain!" she cried.

He put an arm around her. "You can always make a desperate effort to escape and force them to kill you. It is

131

better if you do that while you are in the care of the women, for I think they would kill you before the men would."

She said, "Haven't you a knife?"

"Not a thing. They took everything."

She whispered, "I have."

He spoke in a very low voice. "How did you get it?"

"I had been cutting meat for our dinner. Will had just come home from the Llano after you were taken and they couldn't find you, and had ridden down to the hayfield. The Indians walked in without a sound. I started to scream, but one of them put his hand over my mouth. I pointed to a pie I had made, and, while they were eating it—they ate like starved wolves—I managed to get this knife and put it in my boot. You take it, Stuart."

"It won't help me. Keep it. If things come to the worst, you can use it on yourself or force them to kill you because of it."

She said, "Stuart, I don't mind if they make fun of the way I look. I know I don't look—feminine, but I don't mind. I just hope you don't think that about me."

"You look beautiful to me in anything," he said.

He remembered then that he had his arm around her, and he let it drop.

She said, "You'd better leave it there, Stuart. It might be the last time."

He put it back. She was firm and solid-feeling. He said, thinking of the time that was left, "How did you come to marry Will?"

She touched his knee for a moment. "I was raised by my father. Mother ran away or something when I was little —I don't know exactly. It was a family scandal. Father was strict and would not let me even talk to a boy. But father died just before I was eighteen, and left me about twenty thousand dollars. I was only a girl, and I guess I wanted to be a hero in the eyes of the town, so I gathered up my money and came to Texas. I ended up at Weatherford because somebody told me it was a good place to go into the cattle business, and that sounded glamorous. Cattle business!" She laughed nervously. "I could see myself going back home as the cattle queen of Texas.

"I took a job teaching French. Then I met Will. He had bought some land scrip and had already located the land, but he didn't have money to stock it. Everybody said it was

132

a good chance to invest, so I offered to put in with him— and then he suggested we might as well get married, since I would want to keep an eye on my money."

"Has he been a good husband?"

"He's done his best. I didn't think he'd be very romantic, but the women told me marriage wasn't romantic anyway, and I thought they were right."

"And you still think so?"

She said slowly, "Until tonight."

His arm tightened around her. "Tonight you think that two persons could stand under the stars with their arms around each other and their lips together and the world could blow up and they would never know it."

"Yes," she said. "How do you know, Stuart?"

"Because I feel that way, too."

He put his other arm around her and kissed her hard. A wave of feeling made him dizzy for a moment. Then he released her and said breathlessly, "If we get out of here, we'll have to forget this."

"I know," she said. "There's nothing else to do."

He kissed her again. "But if we don't get out of here alive—"

He heard Big Knife and Cottonwood Leaf returning and took his arms from around her. "It's a strange time to make love," he said, "but, if it hadn't been for this, we never would have told each other."

"I'm glad, Stuart—terribly glad."

More steps came from the darkness, and the grating voice of Stone Calf said: "You make up your mind to lead us to the cache, Many Mules?"

Stuart said slowly, "I haven't decided."

"You have a chance to talk together."

"Yes."

Stone Calf said, "It is as I suspected. You are in love with each other."

Stuart did not answer.

Stone Calf said, "You would lead us to the cache before you would watch my warriors cover her one after another, wouldn't you?"

Stuart jumped to his feet. "Stone Calf, she has nothing to do with the lead or the war."

Stone Calf said easily, "Sit down, Many Mules. Big Knife is at your back with the bowie knife. I have told him not to

133

use it to kill you, because I want you to stay alive—but it can hurt if it goes into your lungs."

Stuart said, "White men can endure as much as an Indian." But he knew it wasn't true.

Stone Calf explained. "It is not that I have any compunction for your life. But in this case, Many Mules, your usefulness to us is considerable, and for that reason only are you alive tonight."

Stuart did not answer.

"And you, Woman Wearing Man Pants, I don't know what you are covering up with such clothes, but I can tell you my warriors will soon find out."

Stuart, trying desperately to avoid any precipitate actions on the part of the Cheyennes, said, in a voice full of scorn, "You are not granting her the dignity you ask for your own people."

Stone Calf laughed. "White men have so many foolish little superstitions. You do not think such things should be said before your women."

"It is bad medicine," said Stuart.

"Medicine!" Stone Calf scoffed. "What could you possibly know of medicine?"

"I have been among many tribes."

"And your only reaction has been that an Indian was to be killed—like a rattlesnake—*she-shin-no-vote!*" Stone Calf's voice was unexpectedly filled with bitterness. "And you know about medicine! Have you ever spent four days and nights on a hillside fasting in the *a-wu-wun?* Have you ever swung from the pole? Have you ever slept on the white sage? Have you ever looked into the blood of a badger to see what your destiny will be? Fah!" Stone Calf was indignant. "And you speak of medicine!"

Stuart kept still.

Big Knife and Cottonwood Leaf came back to see what the talking was about.

Stone Calf said, "He is talking now like a *ve-ah-o* who has whisky to trade for buffalo robes. He is a smart *ve-ah-o*. He knows all about medicine and power and perhaps the taboos, also. He is a smart white man. He knows many things. Also he knows where the lead is, and he will be glad to tell us before the sun comes up." He stopped for a moment in his indignation—or perhaps in frustration because Stuart had not

134

already agreed to tell. "Watch them both," he said to Big Knife. "I go to prepare the lodge. When the Big Dipper points to midnight, bring them to my tepee."

He stalked away.

CHAPTER XX

STUART was silent as he watched the Cheyennes begin to drift toward Stone Calf's tepee. They could not go inside, for Stone Calf had called the old medicine man and they were purifying the tepee with smoke from the white sage, cedar bark and many sprinklings of the various powders which Broken Antelope Horn produced from his buckskin bags.

In between, one would mutter prayers and incantations and the other would answer. They were going through a long ritual which, Stuart knew, boded ill—for the longer the ritual, the more important was the event about to take place. And although the business of trying to make a captive talk was not one that called for medicine as a rule, they were going to extreme lengths to assure themselves of success.

He watched the stars and knew it was near midnight. Stone Calf and Broken Antelope Horn had been joined by two others, and now the sacred number—four—were engaged in purifying and cleansing the tepee. Several others waited outside.

The smell of cedar bark was strong in the village, and Stuart thought that more than one of the warriors had made some private medicine for this affair. It was an indication of the importance of the lead. They wanted no failure.

Stuart said in a low voice, "About the time they're ready for me, we might be able to make a run for it. Can you make out a path to the west rim?"

Anne sounded as if she was shivering when she said, "Somebody came down about half an hour ago, just to the right."

Stuart felt sure, then, that the guards were gone from the rim. Cottonwood Leaf had gone into her tepee. Big Knife probably was somewhere behind Anne and him.

"If we could get up there during the night, we could travel quietly and be several miles away by dawn. Then, perhaps, we would run into soldiers."

He did not tell her that he did not think they would be able to escape. He felt he owed it to her to try, that it was something they *must* try before giving up to what lay ahead of them both. He did not add, either, that he was sure they would not have more than half an hour after the first gray showed in the east.

"I'll try," she whispered.

He said, "When I start something, you run. I'll come behind you."

The village was very quiet. The only light was a red glow from Stone Calf's tepee. The dogs apparently were asleep, and even the horses had not awakened for their one o'clock grazing. The only sounds were the incessant buzzing of the crickets and the steady croak of the frogs—and against that background the intermittent, singsong cadence of the men in the tepee.

Stuart saw the stars indicate midnight. He took hold of Anne's arm and squeezed it briefly. Big Knife was directly behind him, and had been motionless for so long that Stuart thought he might be asleep. He got his legs under him carefully and leaped to his feet like a rearing horse, aiming with the top of his head for Big Knife's chin.

Anne flashed to her feet and ran around the tepee.

Stuart's head hit nothing. Then the back of the heavy blade crashed down on the top of his head. He heard Anne scream, and then he lost consciousness.

A moment later, he was shaking his head to clear it. Anne was coming back around the tepee, Cottonwood Leaf behind her. Big Knife grunted a couple of times.

Stuart felt blood running down the back of his head. He was sure he had a long cut in his scalp, but he did not tempt Big Knife by feeling the wound. Big Knife, with his youth and vitality, might like to try his arm out again on Stuart's head.

Cottonwood Leaf said, "You try to escape, Woman Wearing Man Pants, and the next time the warriors will take charge of you."

Anne said, in despair, "Why don't you kill me and get it over with?"

Cottonwood Leaf shrugged. Her bronze face barely reflected the light from Stone Calf's tepee. "The warriors would accuse me of jealousy."

Stuart understood, though somewhat vaguely. To be accused of a characteristic such as jealousy, greediness or unforgivingness was, in the Cheyenne mind, a derogation hard to live down. Cottonwood Leaf didn't mind killing, but being accused of jealousy was more than she could face.

Stone Calf's voice came from the tepee. Stuart did not hear what he said, but Big Knife seized him by the neck of his shirt and pulled him off the ground.

Stuart started toward the tepee. He heard Anne behind him.

He stopped at the entrance, and Big Knife grunted. Stuart stooped and stepped inside.

Stone Calf motioned. There was a twelve-inch cottonwood stump between the fire and the entrance of the tepee, and Big Knife pushed Stuart down on the ground before the stump.

Stone Calf motioned again. Big Knife said something behind Stuart, and Anne came in and stood just inside the door.

This was most unusual, Stuart thought—for a woman to be present at any sort of ceremony. Perhaps her wearing pants was the justification used by Stone Calf.

Stuart stared at the bronze faces across the fire from him. He realized that all the talk, the thinking, the bravado of his defying Stone Calf, all the things that Stone Calf had done, were but a prelude to the actual decision he must make of telling or not telling where the lead was or how they could find it. And he realized that until now that decision had not been real to him.

If he did not agree, if he found himself able to stand the torture, even then he would have to watch Anne raped time after time—and he did not delude himself—those Cheyennes would be as brutal at that as they were at anything else.

He felt the sweat pouring down his back as he thought about it. Anne had said she could not stand pain.

He felt an impulse to shout at Stone Calf that he was ready to talk. What had he to gain by keeping still? Loving Anne as he did, he knew that whatever torture they might inflict on him would be nothing to their torture and degradation of her. And for what? Would anybody else go through with it to keep the Indians from being able to fight the solders? Couldn't the soldiers look out for themselves? Were ordinary civilians supposed to endure the tortures of the damned to make it easier for Miles's men?

He looked up at Anne and swallowed. One look of terror from her and he would have talked. But she stared at Stone Calf, and there was no terror in her eyes. Her face was white and the scratches on it were livid, but every feature was firm in defiance. Her small hands were clenched, and her body was rigid. Fear was in her face, but not terror. Her lips were a tight line and her eyes narrow as she stared back at Stone Calf and his warriors.

Stuart looked back across the fire at the nine warriors. All were watching Anne, and Stuart knew they were anticipating much more than learning the whereabouts of the lead.

Big Knife closed the entrance of the lodge and tied it with rawhide. He went over and sat down at Stone Calf's left. Anne was still standing. Stuart, sitting on the floor before the stump, looked up at the ten bronze-faced men. They were naked from the waist up, save for the embroidered bands above their elbows. Most of them had one or two feathers in their hair. Big Knife had three, two with blood on them, indicating feats of valor and perhaps wounds.

Aside from Stone Calf and Broken Antelope Horn and Buffalo Tail, not a warrior there was over eighteen, and there was no pity or sympathy or any feeling of sentiment in any one of them.

Stone Calf filled his long-stemmed pipe with tobacco from a buckskin bag. Broken Antelope Horn got up and caught a coal between two twigs. Stone Calf drew on the pipe and got it lighted. Broken Antelope Horn sat down.

Stone Calf sat immovable for a few minutes, looking at nothing. Finally he pointed the pipestem to the sky and said, "Spirit Above, smoke." He pointed it to the ground and said, "Earth, smoke." He pointed it east and said, "East, smoke." In between each motion he puffed on the pipe and blew the smoke from his mouth in a long stream.

He handed it to Big Knife, who went through the same ritual. Big Knife handed it to the man at his left. That man smoked, and then the pipe was handed around the semi-circle to Buffalo Tail, who sat at the extreme right of Stone

Calf. He smoked and handed it to Broken Antelope Horn at his left. Presently it went back to Stone Calf.

Stone Calf took the pipe again, sprinkled some dust on the tobacco, and recited a long and solemn prayer in Cheyenne.

This occupied at least half an hour, and by that time Stuart began to feel half hypnotized by the strange surroundings and the repetition of the movements and the words, but not in such a way as to allay the feeling of suspense and awful dread that had been building up within him for several hours. His skin was hot and dry; his face felt drawn; his throat seemed to be closing up while his stomach felt like a hard knot. Stone Calf's grating voice went on and on.

Finally Stone Calf laid aside the pipe and said, "This man has been captured by our warriors and is said to know where there is lead for many bullets. We have prayed to the Great Spirit and have asked his guidance, and the signs are good. The medicine is right and it is strong. The Great Spirit has assured us that what we are about to do is good and that it will help the Cheyenne to keep the land that is theirs by right of usage through many generations. The Great Spirit has told us that the Cheyenne and the Comanche are destined to drive the white man from the plains. The buffalo will return in countless numbers. Our children will no longer cry for food, and our warriors will not—suffer the degradation of begging for food from the hand of a white man."

Stuart swallowed hard as he wondered exactly what was coming.

Stone Calf said, "Many Mules, you have heard the voice of the Great Spirit through this lodge. You have seen the justice of the Cheyenne's course. You have been promised freedom for yourself and for the Woman Wearing Man Pants if you lead us to the cache of lead that will enable us to win the war. Have you made a decision?"

Stuart took a deep breath. "I'm not going to do it," he said, and he knew there never had been any decision to make.

Stone Calf nodded. Buffalo Tail and Big Knife got up. Stone Calf said, "Put your tongue on the stump, Many Mules."

Stuart shook his head.

Stone Calf said through narrowed eyes, "Do you want me to go into your mouth after your tongue, Many Mules?"

Stuart bit his lip. They wanted the lead first and foremost; but they had worked themselves up to an emotional state that was almost in the nature of a fanatical frenzy. If he

140

refused to put out his tongue, it could be that Stone Calf would decide to cut away his jaw to get at it. At any rate, whatever was to come, he knew it would be less horrible if he could keep them from the burst of violence and cruelty that was lying just beneath the surface. He leaned forward and put his tongue out on the block as far as he could, for he didn't want them to tear it out.

In one swift movement Buffalo Tail drove a slim knife through the center of it and pinned it to the stump.

For a moment the blood rushed to his head and he thought he would faint from the pain, but through the wavering haze he fixed his gaze on Stone Calf's slitted eyes, remembering his hate and keeping the bronze face in his sight.

Anne screamed, and he started to turn to reassure her, but the sharp knife, driven in with the blade outward, cut a fiery path in his tongue. He did not finish turning around but looked again at Stone Calf.

"You may pull back," said Stone Calf, "and you will have a split tongue. But to be sure you do not pull back without wishing it—for I perceive Many Mules is not as unflinching as Big Knife—I will have a man at your back to hold your head in place."

He felt Buffalo Tail's knee against the back of his head, and two warriors came up, one to hold each arm before him. Now he was unable to move or even to turn his head. It seemed more like a fantasy than ever, except that the pain in his tongue was overpowering. Then the wave of dizziness passed and left him nauseated.

Stone Calf said, "What is your answer, Many Mules?"

Stuart stared at him, hating him, wishing he were free to choke him.

Big Knife stood at his right, the bowie knife poised in his hand. The Indian's face was expressionless but his black eyes gleamed with cruelty.

Stone Calf saw the hatred in Stuart's face, for he nodded as Stuart turned his eyes back to him. And almost before he saw the nod, the big blade flashed before Stuart's face. He heard it swish through the air and smack as it bit into the stump. Then Big Knife pulled the knife out of the wood, lifting at first one end and then the other, for it had gone in a half inch.

From the sudden numbness in the end of his tongue, followed by an excruciating pain that was, for the moment, far

141

sharper than that caused by the knife pinning his tongue to the stump, Stuart realized that the end of his tongue had been cut off. Probably it was only a small piece, for it would be an essential part of Stone Calf's program to make this last as long as possible. In a moment the pain seemed to hit him at the back of the neck like a physical blow and then travel upward, spreading through his head in a dizzying wave of heat and pain.

Then the pain at the end of his tongue made itself felt like the searing of a hot iron, and he jerked back instinctively, only to feel and hear the slim knife cutting through the hard gristle of his tongue. He moved his head forward again.

All this must have happened in a second, for then he heard Anne scream, "Stuart! Tell him!"

Through the haze of pain he glared at Stone Calf, and the hard, expressionless face with the slitted eyes made him furious above the throbbing pain. He could not talk but he could think, "Go ahead, you red-skinned son-of-a-bitch! Cut it all off and be done with it!"

Stone Calf saw the defiance in his eyes and nodded again. Again the heavy blade flashed, and there was a repetition of the pain. This time it left him weak and sick at his stomach. It took all his strength to control the vomiting movements of his throat.

Anne was screaming hysterically. Stuart heard scuffling behind him as she was flung to the floor. For an instant she was silent, and Stuart heard everyone's harsh breathing. For a moment, he thought the frenzy had reached its peak and the Cheyennes were about to attack her, but Stone Calf drew a deep breath and shook his head. He sat for a moment, and little by little the wild light died in his own eyes.

The pain returned. Stuart's tongue seemed to be intolerably big, and every drop of blood in it ached beyond endurance. But through the blur of the agony he heard Stone Calf speaking.

"Many Mules, we want to find the lead. If you agree to help us, we will turn you and the woman loose and allow you to go home unmolested."

Anne began to sob hysterically.

"If you do not talk now, you will never be able to talk again—and I will not be responsible for the Woman Wearing Man Pants."

It was hard to think through the haze of pain. He knew he

142

might have to go through life speechless, and he guessed he could face that—but brutality and torment to Anne seemed more than he could possibly bear. And he knew that if this went much further, not even Stone Calf would be able to control his warriors.

He closed his eyes for a moment, then gave up. He opened his eyes and looked at Stone Calf. For a moment he thought he had waited too long, for the beginnings of frenzy were on Stone Calf's face once more. Then reluctance came into Stone Calf's eyes. The Cheyenne took a deep breath, and Stuart, pinned to the stump, held almost immovable by the Indians behind him, felt a chill of premonition.

But Stone Calf was not a great chief for nothing. He gained control of the surges of desire that showed plainly on his face and moistened his lips, and the gleam of cruelty died in his eyes. "The Cheyenne keeps his word," he said in his grating voice. He nodded.

Buffalo Tail took hold of the knife that held Stuart's tongue pinned down and jerked it out of the stump. Automatically, Stuart pulled his dry tongue back into his warm mouth. But there was no tip on his tongue, no feeling in it, no way to feel with it—just pain. The blood tasted salty and sickening, but he conquered his nausea and got to his feet.

Anne had raised herself on her arms and was looking at him. The fear was gone from her face, and it was strained and white. Her eyes were filled with unutterable relief as she said softly, "Oh, Stuart!"

Stone Calf stood up. At that moment there was a ripping sound that sounded like a sharp knife cutting into a watermelon. Stuart raised his eyes from Anne and saw the great slit in the tepee wall. Then the dew cloth moved suddenly and Will Schooler walked from behind it. He had a knife in one hand, a six-shooter in the other.

"Get her out, Nichols!" His voice was calm, clear and hard. "I'll hold 'em off!"

143

CHAPTER XXI

STUART stared at the sandy-haired man for only the fraction of an instant. As Will Schooler stood inside the tepee, covering the Indians with his pistol, he was a complete man for probably the first time in his life. There was assurance in his manner, authority in his voice. He was a man with death at his fingertips, and he expected to be obeyed.

For a moment even the savages were taken aback by Schooler's commanding appearance. He was hatless, and his thin red hair rose in wisps from the top of his head.

Stone Calf's eyes narrowed until even the slits were almost invisible, but Stuart knew the Cheyennes would be immobile for only a few seconds. He bent over, pulled Anne roughly but without hesitation to her feet. She glanced once at Will, and Stuart thought for a moment she might go to pieces. Then she said, "Will, I'll always remember," and stepped to the entrance of the tepee. At that same moment the tent was slit from outside, and Anne went through the opening. Stuart followed quickly. He heard Utah's voice: "Git on the horses!"

Stuart said thickly, "Give me a gun!"

Utah pressed a six-shooter in his hand, and Stuart swung back to the opening.

He heard Utah say urgently, "Git in the saddle, Miz Schooler, but don't ride till I tell you!"

He pulled back one side of the entrance and held the six-shooter at his waist.

Broken Antelope Horn moved toward Schooler, and Stuart shot him in the chest. The old man crumpled.

144

The sound of the shot, the acrid smell of powder smoke, brought Big Knife back to awareness. He and Buffalo Tail leaped for Schooler at the same time.

Stuart shot Buffalo Tail, and the Cheyenne skidded on his face into the fire, throwing sparks over the interior of the tepee.

Big Knife was in mid-air, his bowie knife aimed at Will Schooler's throat. Schooler shot him three times in the chest, and then Stuart shot him in the left side. But the Indian lived long enough to drive his great knife through Will Schooler's neck.

Two others were converging on Stuart. He fired at each of them and spun on his heel.

Reins were thrust in his hands. The horse started off, and he mounted with a desperate leap. He heard horses thunder through the village ahead of him, and it seemed that the entire valley was echoing with pistol shots.

Stuart didn't try to guide the horse but let it have its head, assuming it would follow the others.

In a moment they had left the village behind and were going north. He had heard no rifle shots, and it was too dark to shoot arrows.

There were at least three horses ahead of him. For a moment he had forgotten about his leg, but now the movement of the horse began to hurt it from front to back. He couldn't use the leg to hang on because it was numb and he couldn't find the stirrup, but he clutched the saddlehorn and balanced the best he could. His tongue ached intolerably and seemed to have swollen until it almost choked him.

They traveled two or three miles at breakneck speed. Then Utah's voice came back: "Slow 'em down."

Stuart was grateful for a rest. The horses came down to a trot. "Miz Schooler, you all right?" asked Utah.

"Yes," she said, "Yes, I'm—all right." She sounded as if she was about ready to fall over.

Utah led them down toward the stream. He called, "Andy! Pablo!"

"*Aquí,*" said Pablo's voice, and they cut the horses down to a walk.

They rode out in a small clearing. Utah struck a match and looked at Stuart's face. "You're pretty white. How do you feel?"

Stuart took a deep breath. "Weak, but let's keep going." He

145

spat out blood. "There'll be all kinds of hell to pay as soon as Stone Calf gets his people organized."

Utah nodded and dropped the match. "We'll move on."

"There's a camp up here on the river. Lieutenant Garner went up there earlier this evening."

Utah, moving away, said, "Let's go."

They moved on north at a trot, but presently slowed down to a walk.

Andy said, "I smell smoke, boss."

Half an hour later a nervous trooper said in a low voice, "Halt! Who goes there?"

"Friends," said Utah.

"Stay where you are until I get the lieutenant."

"We won't move," said Utah. "If you're pointin' a rifle at us, don't get nervous."

The guard called, "Lieutenant Garner!" There was some muffled swearing, but presently the lieutenant called to them in the darkness, "Who's out there?"

Utah said, "Four men and a woman from the Rocking Seven."

The lieutenant said, "Walk your horses in slow so I can see you. Don't make any false moves. I've got a bunch of green men."

They moved across the last two hundred yards of the sandy river bottom. The lieutenant held up a lantern. "Mr. Nichols?"

Stuart nodded.

"Come on in," Garner said, sounding relieved.

The lieutenant examined Stuart's tongue. "I reckon you're all right, but you sure need a doctor. How does it feel?"

Stuart said gruffly, "Hurts my tongue like hell to talk."

"Now bring me up to date," Garner said. "What's been going on?"

"Well," said Utah, "after them Injuns stole Stuart, you remember we split up. You was goin' to try to follow the trail. Pablo and me went with you, and sent the rest back to the Tesecato. Will Schooler kinda got cold feet and decided to go back, too. Fisher went back for reasons of his own."

"And we lost the trail," said Garner.

Utah said morosely, "Them damn' Injuns was mighty smart. They made for the breaks south of the Canadian River, and we lost 'em in a hurry. So me and Pablo went back home to

146

git more help. I figgered if Stuart was able to send word, he would send it to the ranch, and we'd better be there."

Garner looked at Anne. "How did the lady get into the fight?"

"When Will Schooler was out in the hayfield, the Cheyennes come and got her and took her up to Stone Calf to be damn' sure of makin' Stuart talk."

"And what happened to Fisher?"

"He went straight on to his ranch. Whatever talkin' he did to Stone Calf was done before we left the Tesecato."

Garner looked at Utah. "And then you—"

"We was gettin' ready to pull out when Will Schooler come and told us Anne was gone. He found enough sign to know it was Indians, but he couldn't figger out why, and I didn't enlighten him. I gathered up Whitey and Pablo, Andy and Dusty, and us and Schooler went down to the Bar W and picked up the trail. This time we followed it, and about sunset we could see we was gettin' close to the valley. Pablo said he knew a way in, so we laid out in the breaks till dark. Then we come down inside."

"No sentries?"

Utah looked into the fire. "They was a couple. You'll find 'em somewhere up there with their throats cut." He paused. "I didn't take time to scalp 'em."

"You had already picked out Stone Calf's tepee?"

Utah nodded. "We could see the tepee against the sky once we got near the village, and then we heard the chief makin' medicine and we begun to work closer to the tepee. Pretty soon we heard Miz Schooler scream, and we knew somethin' was goin' on. Will Schooler was goin' crazy, but he kep' control of himself, and we all moved together. Then we heard her say, 'Stuart!' and we knew they were both there. I went around to the front with Whitey. Will Schooler went to the side, an' when I gave the signal he ripped the tent open —an' I will say he done magnificent."

Stuart said slowly, "He was every bit a man when he stepped into that tepee."

Then he told them what had happened inside. He talked slowly, painfully and thickly.

The lieutenant asked, "Any chance Schooler is alive?"

Utah shook his head. "He was dead when the Cheyenne fell on him. I saw it. He used that knife like an axe. The Cheyenne was dead, too, but he wouldn't die till he had killed his enemy. Will Schooler shot him three times and Stuart shot him once, and I swear all shots was either in his heart or mighty nigh to it."

"They're hard to kill at close quarters," said the lieutenant.

Stuart saw the fire swaying back and forth like a lamp hanging on a chain. He tried to move to keep it straight, and then he fell over.

He was lying on a blanket when he opened his eyes. He felt numb all over, and his tongue ached until he didn't think he could stand it. He turned his head to spit out blood.

The lieutenant said, "You need a doctor bad. Think you can stand the ride to Colonel Miles's headquarters?"

"I don't know of any closer place," said Stuart, but he wondered how he'd make it.

They started out at dawn. Stuart's tongue was swollen and even cool coffee was agony, but his leg felt a little better. The lieutenant sent out scouts, who reported that Stone Calf's village was gone completely.

Lieutenant Garner looked up at the scout who had come from the site of the village. "Did you find the red-haired white man who was killed in Stone Calf's tent?"

The soldier looked around and saw Anne up in the lead. "Yes, sir—what was left of him. They scalped him and cut off his nose and ears and gouged out his eyes. They cut off his arms and legs and his privates and threw 'em all over the rocks. The coyotes was worryin' the pieces. We run them off an' put the pieces together and buried him in a crack in the rocks."

"If she asks about it," said the lieutenant—and his voice was hard—"just tell her you found his body and buried it."

"Yes, sir."

They reached Miles's camp late that day and started off to the Tesecato early the next morning with a detail of twenty-four men. The lieutenant had made arrangements for a wagon to follow them the next day.

They rode through the Tesecato, and Anne stopped off at the ranch. Stuart got a gun-belt and rifle, and they picked up Dusty and left Whitey and Andy. Stuart went out to the corral that evening and stared at the empty breaking pen. "What happened to the *moro*?"

"He hurt hisself on a fence pole," said Dusty, "and we turned him out in the pasture till you got back."

They started out to find the lead before dawn the next morning, and, when the sun came up, they were on the Llano. Pablo said, "Lots of Indian sign up here."

"They've been scouring the plains," said the lieutenant, "but the Llano is too wide and the big storm swept everything clean. Think you can find it, Mr. Nichols?"

"I think so. Can you get it out of the ground?"

"Our engineers say to build a fire on top of it, and as fast as it melts and run down, to pry off the pieces. It will take time, but we'll get it that way."

Stuart nodded. He was watching the sun.

"How are you goin' to know?" asked Utah.

Stuart said, "I picked up one of those big tumbleweeds and jammed it down on a bear grass so the dead stem of the bear grass stuck up through the middle. The stickers on the bear grass went up into the tumbleweed and stuck in it enough places to hold it. I figured that would last till kingdom come and three dry days."

The lieutenant was beaming. "I believe it would. And nobody would pay any attention if they didn't know. It would just seem to be another tumbleweed caught in a bear grass."

CHAPTER XXII

THEY found it in late afternoon. Stuart grinned, and the lieutenant pounded him on the back. Utah said, "By the great horn spoon, I never rode sign on nothin' like that before."

Stuart said, "Well, Lieutenant, it's all yours. You can spend the next week or the next month getting it out—but it's all yours unless the Cheyennes catch you."

"We've got the one thing they lack," said the lieutenant. "They'll never be able to drive us away from it."

Stuart said, "I feel kind of sorry for the Indians."

The lieutenant nodded. "There are others who do, too."

"They're fighting hard, they're fighting the only way they know, and they're fighting for the only thing they ever had—the land they always lived on. Of course the Cheyennes didn't live on it as much as the Comanches and Kiowas, but nevertheless they lived on land like it, and they were run off of that."

The lieutenant nodded. "Well, you'll want to get back. Going tonight?"

Stuart looked at the sun. "It's close to sunset. I guess we better rest overnight and start back in the morning."

"You're welcome."

Later that night, the lieutenant asked, "You decided to let the law take its course with Fisher?"

Stuart didn't answer immediately. He thought of all the things Fisher was already responsible for and which he would go on doing as long as he was allowed to. There would be

150

conniving with the Indians, with outlaws or with somebody, as long as Fisher saw a chance to come out ahead.

Stuart was tired. His leg ached whenever he was in the saddle; his tongue was slow healing, and seemed to open up every time he talked, ate or drank water. It felt pretty good in the morning, but within a couple of hours it would swell up and create an ache that seemed to encompass his entire throat.

He took a deep breath. "I reckon that would be the sensible thing to do," he said quietly. "But maybe I'm not in shape to be sensible."

They got back into the Tesecato a little before noon.

Anne had insisted on going home. "Can't figure out what got into her," said George. "She was powerful set on leaving the very next morning. Said she had work to do." He looked curiously at Stuart. "You and her had words or something?"

"In a way," said Stuart. He knew what it meant—with Will gone, he would have to make the first move.

"We, got lots of work," said George.

"What do we need first?"

"We better haul some hay and salt up under the western Caprock. We'll have a norther some of these days and then we won't have enough hands to go around."

"All right. We've still got a wagon left, haven't we?"

"One with a box, one with just the running gear."

"All right. Start Utah and Whitey at putting a bed on the gear."

"You're gonna put in a claim for the wagons and mules you lost, aren't you? I heard the Indians burned the wagons."

"Yes. I'll have to go to Dodge about the first for grub, and I'll turn in my claim then."

"You got somethin' on your mind now?"

Stuart took a drink from the dipper. "I'm going to bring the *moro* back to the corral."

Stuart got on the gray. He rode north first and saw that the spring was still going strong. The cottonwoods had shed their leaves, and the grass was beginning to turn dry. The touch of fall was in the air; it wouldn't be long before the north wind would sweep down through the Tesecato, and they would be glad they were not up on the Caprock.

He stopped to help Andy and Slim with a bloated cow. Slim thought she had gotten some kind of poison weed, but

151

they stuck her between the ribs and let out the air, and she seemed to feel better.

He found a horse that had been eating loco. The hair on its flanks was long and woolly, and its neck was thin and mangy. Stuart shot it in one ear and left it for the coyotes.

It was late afternoon by the time Stuart and Utah started for the lower pasture where they had put the *moro*. The pasture led into a long sliver of land that ran alongside the Bar M and touched Fisher's property at the far end.

Stuart rode out away from the Schooler ranch house, trying to keep out of sight of it in the bear grass, scrub oak and cedars. He came out on the point that marked the end of his land, still without seeing the *moro*. He looked around, puzzled. He saw sign but no horse.

And then, over on Fisher's property, Stuart heard the terrifying scream of a hurt horse. He stared for an instant. A horse bucked out of some tall mesquite. It was the mulberry-colored stallion, and on its back was Fisher, who was holding a halter rope and beating the horse at every jump with a short-handled whip.

They were half a mile away. He heard Fisher's foul curses and saw the frantic leaps of the horse as it tried to throw the man off. He could not quite understand why the horse was so crazy. It had been skittery with him but never the way it was now.

Stuart broke into a dead gallop, heading directly across the open country. The *moro* turned his way, and Fisher apparently looked up and saw him, for he seemed to stare for a moment. Then the *moro* hit Fisher, tossed him high in the air and continued to buck toward the Caprock.

Stuart's blood was boiling, but he hesitated at going after Fisher immediately, for the *moro* was still bucking. Stuart hadn't figured it to be that kind of horse. The *moro* reached the Caprock and turned north, bucking among the rocks, squealing and screaming in terror—or agony.

Stuart cut back to intercept it. The horse was bucking blind and didn't even see him approach. He rode alongside and felt a chill down his backbone when he saw what had been done— Fisher had twisted a fine brass wire around the horse's lower jaw and left it there.

Stuart was torn between going after Fisher and relieving the *moro* of its pain. There was only one answer. He shook out a loop, roped the *moro* by its hind legs and threw it. Utah galloped up, and Stuart pointed. Utah swore. Stuart sat on the *moro's* neck, and Utah brought the pliers from his saddlebag. They cut the wire and unwound it from the horse's jaw; then Stuart stroked its neck until it calmed down. Then they let it up and Stuart mounted the gray.

"Where you goin'?" asked Utah.

Stuart looked off across the canyon. "I'm going to kill that son-of-a-bitch," he said quietly.

Utah looked up at the Caprock. It was almost dark. He said, "You better take some help."

The anger in Stuart was intense, but there was flat deadliness in his voice.

"I don't need help. I'll take care of Fisher, and it will be as brutal as what he did to the *moro*. I don't want anybody watching it."

He checked his six-shooter and saw that there were five cartridges in it.

He watched the purples and reds and browns of the eastern Caprock, now deep in shadows and softened and muted by the dusk. A nighthawk, swooping somewhere above them, uttered its single-noted buzzing chirrup. From far to the south came a scream that sounded like a woman in terror.

Stuart jerked. Utah said, "We better get that panther before next spring."

Stuart nodded.

Utah pointed. "Pablo and Dusty are up there workin' the swamp."

"They should be headed home by now."

A yellow light appeared in the kitchen window of the Schooler place. A coyote barked up on the west rim. Stuart straightened up in the saddle.

"How do you feel now?" asked Utah.

"No different."

"Then you better get it over with—but you might as well know—the whole crew is watchin'. They knew this was goin' to happen, for Fisher tried to ride the *moro* once when you was gone. They're all up there in the swamp with rifles, waitin' for you to start south."

Stuart said, "That ain't necessary. It's my fight."

"We don't aim to interfere with you and Fisher. It's only that if his hands step in, we want to sort of even up the odds."

Stuart said, "I don't like for anybody else to be in it, but

153

it looks as if I've got to kill him personally. Nobody knows what he'll be up to next—and right now we're six months away from a sheriff."

"That's what George said."

Stuart looked questioningly at him. "I thought George wanted me to wait for the law."

"He wanted you to, all right—but that doesn't mean he figured it would be best that way."

"With Anne there on the ranch alone—" Stuart's jaws tightened grimly. "Stay back as long as you can," he said. "Maybe Fisher's hands will keep out of it."

"We'll watch," said Utah, "but we ain't superhuman, and the army is busy with Indians."

Stuart rode off at a lope, followed at a distance by his men.

He cut across the grass flat and got into the darker area along the creek. There was no moon, but the stars were beginning to come out. On the west, the great silhouette of the Caprock showed as a massive range of hills.

He saw Fisher's low adobe up ahead and slowed down. It was dark, no lights anywhere. Stuart didn't like it. He heard horses milling. The gray stretched its neck to neigh, but he got his fingers over the horse's nostrils and stopped it.

He rode in under a cottonwood tree and sat the gray there for a minute, getting his bearings. Then he dismounted, ground-tied the gray and started on foot for the front door.

A bullet cracked past him. The yellow explosion blinded him for a moment. Then the dull boom of the powder reached his ears, and after it the whine of the bullet as it ricocheted across the valley.

"Come on out, Fisher," he called. "I've got business with you."

That time he moved as he spoke. At least three bullets cut through the place where he had been.

He went back to move the gray to an *arroyada*.

"Do we storm the place," called Utah, "or do we go home and think about it?"

There was only one answer to that. This man had betrayed them to the Indians; he had set the Indians on them; he had taken Stuart's horse and tortured it. What was left? The man was loco and was apparently surrounded by a bunch of hands who would back him up. The next thing that happened, the Indians would attack from the north and Fisher from the

154

south, and then Fisher would have the whole Tesecato to himself. Somebody had to call his hand. Stuart turned to the men. "We'll take the place, since he won't come out. Keep covered as much as you can. Try not to get hurt. It may be we can surround the house and force him out."

"The corrals are off to the right," Utah said.

They came out on the hard-packed bare dirt of the yard and began to move on their toes. Utah was carrying his carbine at his side. Dusty had his rifle cradled in his arms.

A voice came from the corrals: "That you, Nichols?"

"Who did you expect?" asked Stuart.

"What are you doin' on my place?"

"I came to give you a whipping like you never had before." Fisher said, "You'll never whip me again, Nichols."

Stuart said, "I don't want to start a range war. You and I can go off and settle this by ourselves."

"There's nothin' to settle," said Fisher. "I caught you in my corral. I can shoot you down and be done with it."

"If it was *you* in *my* corral, the answer is yes."

"You'd shoot me, wouldn't you?" said Fisher.

Stuart said harshly, "Maybe I'd hang you to a cottonwood tree."

"That's a good idea," said Fisher. "Maybe *I'll* hang *you*."

Stuart was trying to spot Fisher, but it was too dark. Dusty was down on one knee, and Stuart pulled away to the right. The rest of them spread out.

Stuart said again, "Come on out, Fisher, and we'll settle it—us two."

Somebody alongside Fisher fired a six-shooter. In the blaze of red and yellow light, Stuart saw Dusty and Utah rolling. Pablo and Slim were on their stomachs. Stuart fired at the light as he moved to one side.

Fisher shot at him as two of Stuart's men fired at Fisher. The yard erupted in a volcanic upheaval of fire, explosions, and acrid smoke. For a moment it was lighted up, and Stuart saw men crouched and running all around the corrals. Then the white smoke closed in and hid them, and the flashes became momentary, like the glow of a firefly. Only the crash of six-shooters and rifles carried the message of violence and death.

It stopped as suddenly as it had started. For a moment there was no sound. Then a stick cracked, and Utah's carbine boomed. Somewhere around the corral, a man choked and fell heavily against the fence.

Stuart had been moving to a rock and was getting close to the ranch house, but he had no doubt somebody was stationed there. He began to move forward. If they could surround the corrals, they might bring a showdown.

He fired and jumped to one side. A rifle answered him. He fired again and jumped, but that time he crashed into a fence. He dropped and rolled as a burst of rifle and six-shooter fire splintered the poles where he had fallen.

Utah and his men were watching. Before the concentrated firing was over, Utah and the other three men poured lead into the red and yellow blazes. One man groaned and fell. One cursed and said, "I'm hit, Fisher—hit bad!"

Stuart, crouched, moved toward the place where the man had groaned. He heard Fisher cursing. Then he got close and said, "All right, Fisher. Swing around shooting or throw away your gun and start throwing fists."

Fisher swung shooting, and his bullet singed Stuart's ear. Then Stuart planted his last bullet square in Fisher's breastbone and stood for a moment as he heard the man go down.

It was quiet then in the ranch yard, and a hoot owl up in the cottonwood tree began to give out its wavery call.

Stuart stood for a moment. It hadn't been brutal; it hadn't been long and drawn out—but it was over now, quickly, and Fisher was dead.

Stuart stood up and called in his thick voice, "Anybody else want to fight?"

After a moment, a voice said, "I've had enough. I was going to Montana anyways."

"Anybody else?" asked Stuart.

Somebody came out of the house. "Our pay has stopped if Fisher is dead," said one.

"All right. Mind your own business."

"Are you takin' us in?"

"I don't want you," said Stuart, "and neither does the Panhandle. You better bury this carcass."

"He isn't our kin," said a voice out of the darkness. "Anyway, he owes me three months' back pay. He can rot right where he is."

Stuart said, "Better light a match and be sure it's Fisher."

"I won't git shot, will I?"

"Not if you do what I say."

A sulphur match flared out. Its smell was stronger than that of the burned gunpowder. Stuart glanced at Fisher's unshaven face, and then up at the long, straggly mustache of the man holding the match. "If you're leaving," he said coldly, "you'd better take your war bag."

"Yes, sir."

He waited until they had all left. Then he walked over to Utah. "Anybody hurt here?" he asked.

Utah got up. "Dusty got one in his arm, but not serious, I guess. The cook can dig it out."

Stuart said, "There ought to be more Fisher hands around."

Utah said, "He never had enough hands. He didn't have any cows. What use did he have for hands?"

Stuart nodded absently. "Let's get along," he said.

"We'll be busy tomorrow," Utah said, turning to the horses. "Somebody will have to come down here and see there isn't any stock penned up in the corrals."

"I'll do that," said Stuart. "But I'll want somebody to help me bury him."

"Buryin's too good for him," said Utah.

Stuart said vehemently, "Anything that ever happened is too good for him."

They rode up toward the Schooler place. "You can go along," said Stuart. "I'm going to stop here for a minute. I want to see how Miz Schooler is getting along."

"Nobody has seen her for a while," Dusty observed.

"She shouldn't be here with nothing but the hands around. She was pretty upset."

"I'll take the men on back and get Dusty's bullet dug out," said Utah.

Stuart rode off the road and into the ranch yard of the Bar M. He went past the bunkhouse where the hands stayed, and saw coal-oil lamps burning in the windows. Two men were playing checkers; one was hanging up socks. He went on to the smaller ranch house. A light showed dimly from the kitchen window. He knocked on the door, self-conscious, and then remembered to say, "Hello."

Anne called out, "Who is it?"

"Stuart Nichols," he said.

"Just a minute." He backed away from the door, still holding the reins of the gray. He saw her cross the window. He waited for a minute, wondering what she was doing, and then got out his Bull Durham and rolled a cigarette. He lighted it and sat on his heels near the back door, smoking and waiting. He was a little tight inside. He tried to tell himself it was from the fight, but he knew better. He was wondering how it would be now with him and Anne.

Finally she rushed past the window before he could see her, opened the door and said, "All right, Stuart, come in."

He walked inside, ducking under the door mantel. Then his eyes got used to the light and he stared at her. She had fixed her brown hair up in curls, and one strand of them hung down on her white neck. She was wearing a pink and white dress. He stared. "Anne, you're beautiful!" he said.

She stood before him, smiling, expectant, waiting, and then he caught her and held her tightly in his arms and felt her tears go through his shirt sleeve.

Outside, it was peaceful and calm. The frogs and the crickets were making their homey sounds, the coyote yapped on the western Caprock and a cow mooed across the road. The night wind drifted in through the open door and sucked out the light, but neither of them noticed, for with them it was calm, too—and peaceful—and tempestuous and heady, and all the things that a man and woman have known together since the beginning of time.

Noel M(iller) Loomis was born in Oklahoma Territory and retained all his life a strong Southwestern heritage. One of his grandfathers made the California Gold Rush in 1849 and another was in the Cherokee Strip land rush in 1893. He grew up in Oklahoma, New Mexico, Texas, and Wyoming, areas in the American West that would figure prominently in his Western stories. His parents operated an itinerant printing and newspaper business and, as a boy, he learned to set lead type by hand. Although he began contributing Western fiction to the magazine market in the late 1930s, it was with publication of his first novel, *Rim of the Caprock* (1952), that he truly came to prominence. This novel is set in Texas, the location of two other notable literary endeavors, *Tejas Country* (1953) and *The Twilighters* (1955). These novels evoke the harsh, even savage violence of an untamed land in a graphic manner that eschewed sharply the romanticism of fiction so characteristic of an earlier period in the literary history of the Western story. In these novels, as well as *West to the Sun* (1955), *Short Cut to Red River* (1958), and *Cheyenne War Cry* (1959), Loomis very precisely sets forth a precise time and place in frontier history and proceeds to capture the ambiance of the period in descriptions, in attitudes responding to the events of the day, and laconic dialogue that etches vivid characters set against these historical backgrounds. In the second edition of *Twentieth Century Western Writers* (1991), the observation is made that Loomis's work was "far ahead of its time. No other Western writer of the 1950s depicts so honestly the nature of the land and its people, and renders them so alive. Avoiding comment, he concentrates on the atmosphere of time and place. One experiences with him the smell of Indian camps and frontier trading posts, the breathtaking vision of the Caprock, the sudden terror of a surprise attack. Loomis, in his swift character sketches, his striking descriptions, his lithe effective style, brings that world to life before our eyes. In the field he chose, he has yet to be surpassed."